FLIGHT OF PASSION LARGE PRINT

LOVE AMONGST THE BUTTERFLIES

MOLLIE MATHEWS

Blue Orchid
PUBLISHING

Flight of
Passion

Mollie Mathews

Blue Orchid Publishing

PRAISE FOR FLIGHT OF PASSION

"This is a well-written book that tantalizes your senses. Will Oliver be able to convince Ruby that she loves him enough to disobey her family? Can they find each other when all seems lost? An excellent book that I highly recommend. It will have you laughing with joy and crying with sadness."

~ **Marie Fraser**

"Mollie Mathews has written a beautifully scripted story of two people wildly attracted to each other but too constrained by family expectations to allow themselves to commit. When they meet again after eight years can they move beyond old patterns of behavior or are they doomed to always want, but never have?"

                                    ~ **Jane Whitmeyer**

"This book is a carefully crafted, truly original story. Mollie's wonderfully descriptive narrative paints a picture in which it is easy to lose oneself—I really felt like I had been to Mexico by the time I had finished. Her butterfly theme echoes throughout the book, both literally and figuratively. The main characters, Oliver and Ruby, are each conflicted in their own ways. Despite facing challenges, both ultimately find the strength to work through their difficulties to emerge better people, and most importantly, triumph over adversity together. A touching and heart-warming book, well worth a read."

                                       ~ **Cathy Rioran**

"Fast-paced, heart-wrenching completely unexpected twists, excellent storyline, and a hell of a good read. You just gotta love Mollie's imagination and expertise in her writing."

                                    ~ **Rae Waterhouse**

"I fell in love with Ruby and Oliver, they are so good for each other, but both are so filled with garbage that their families filled them with, that they can't see what's in front of them. And when they finally realize that diamonds don't have a hold to what they had, they are about to lose it. The butterflies remind me of how ethereal life is and it is up to us to not waste it, but live the fullest and best we can."

~ **Advance reviewer**

"I really enjoyed Flight of Passion! I loved the descriptions of the butterflies and of the setting of the farm in Mexico. Wonderfully descriptive writing that transports you to a golden orchard filled with butterflies. Perfect for a cold winter's evening curled up by the fire."

~ **Linda Buckhingham**

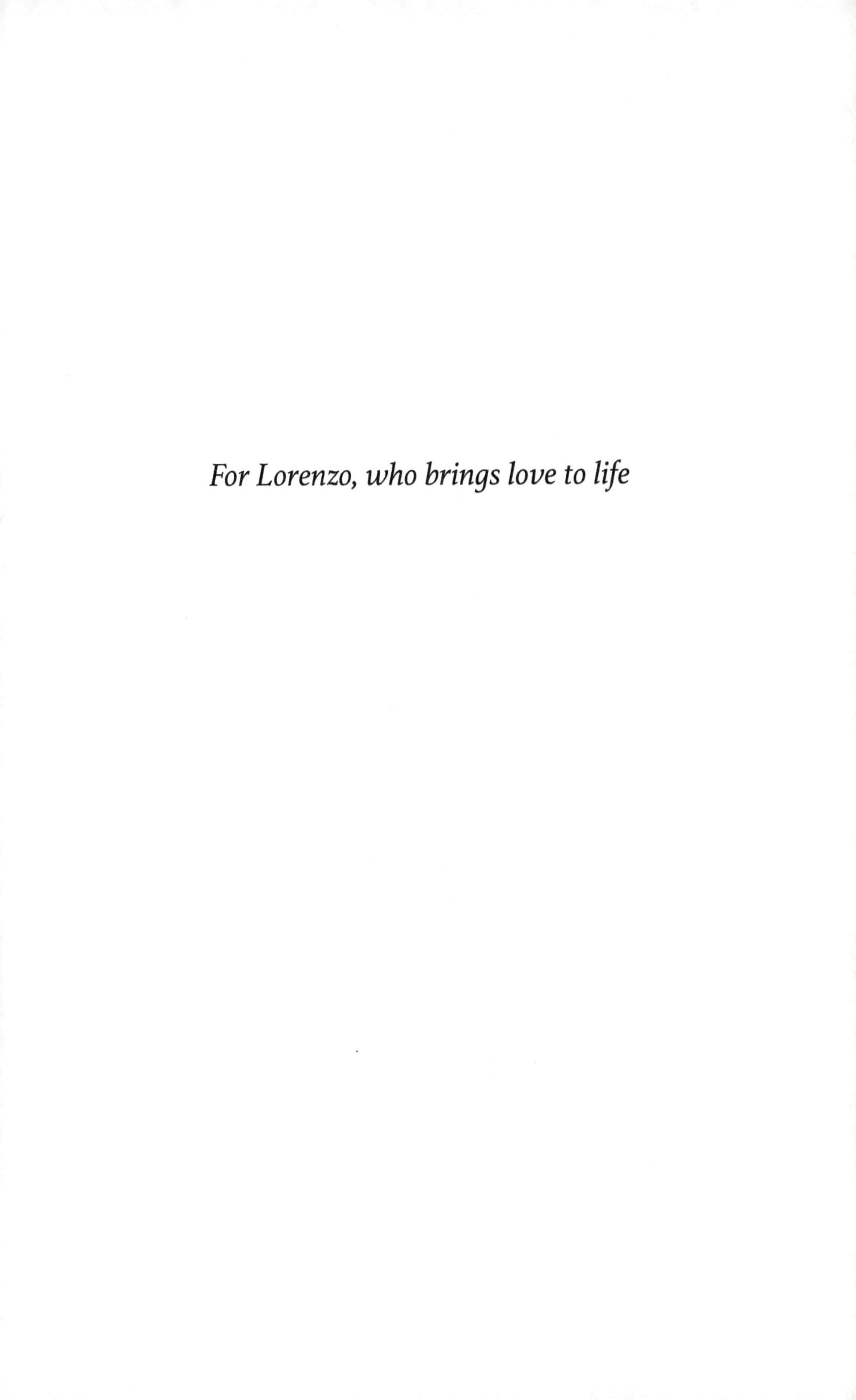

For Lorenzo, who brings love to life

PROLOGUE

G ROWING UP OLIVER WAS LEFT WITH THE impression he wasn't worthy. First by his parents who at the age of four sent him to the bottom of the world. It was as if they didn't know what to do with their infinitely curious and energetic child. It was as if sending him to the most prestigious boarding school in New Zealand absolved them of their responsibility, the responsibility which was every parents'—or should be, he thought bitterly—to love their child unconditionally.

After his run-in with a box of matches, they told him he would amount to nothing. He proved them wrong. At sixteen, he left New Zealand and headed for New York. It was true. If he could make it there, he could make it anywhere. With the ruthless determination he was both admired and feared for, like King Kong on steroids, he quickly climbed to the top of the property acquisition tree.

He was king of the beasts, the man everyone wanted at their dreary New York parties, full of checkbook philanthropists who would never stoop to get close to the people their showy donations benefitted. Parties, like the one where he'd first met Ruby Diaz

Ruby had fluttered into his life like a breath of fresh air. She had lit up the room with her illuminating presence and dazzlingly rare beauty—not just on the outside but the inside too. Her authenticity had the scent of violets—too guileless for pretense.

His darling Ruby. Oliver swallowed hard, refusing to succumb to the wave of angry hurt that swum from his heart to his throat.

For three blissful years, they were inseparable. But no matter how much success Oliver acquired, how extraordinarily wealthy he became, Oliver wasn't good enough for the Diaz's darling Ruby. He never knew why she flew from his life, disappearing as quickly as she'd arrived. She had said nothing, given him no explanation, not even the courtesy of a call.

The Diaz family and the way Ruby had callously abandoned him reminded Oliver he would never be worthy—he was unlovable. Perhaps he should thank them for sparing him further hurt. Thanks to them and his hopeless parents, he swore never to love again.

And that suited him just fine.

OBSESSION

I would like to be the air that inhabits you

~ Margaret Atwood ~

1

WOULD SELLING *BUTTERFLY LOVERS* REALLY free him of painful memories he'd rather forget?

Common sense told Oliver Hart that *Butterfly Lovers* was just a painting. An inanimate object, incapable of controlling him. But that was the trouble—it did control him, seducing him with its beauty, twisting his heart with bittersweet memories.

He'd intended to keep it . . . her . . . forever. His heartbeat seemed to almost stop as he thought of Ruby Diaz, the woman who had inspired the painting's commission. He rubbed his powerful chest, trying to ease the painful tightness that constricted his lungs as he surveyed the crowd gathered for the charity art auction.

It was time to let them both go. But would Oliver ever be free?

His gaze swept over the minimalist, exquisitely designed interior, lingering over the priceless abstract by Rothko adorning a charcoal-black wall, at Hillcrest, his newly acquired mansion, and New Jersey's most expensive country estate.

Tonight, though, it was *Butterfly Lovers* which held in its grip women dripping with diamonds, and men clad in Armani. Locked in shared awe, they clustered around the painting, studying every line, every pulsating color.

Oliver wondered if their eyes ached as his did with a heady mix of pleasure and pain just to stand in its spellbinding presence. Or were they trying to decode the painting's hidden secrets?

Like a moth to a seductive flame, his eyes drifted to the bottom of the painting. Nobody, but one other person, would ever be able to decipher the graffiti-style line of poetry scrawled in throbbing orange along the bottom of the painting.

Painful memories bled into his consciousness. Why the hell couldn't he shake her?

Butterfly Lovers. The painting was aptly named, he mused, forcing his mind from the woman who had inspired the purchase. The dancing kaleidoscope of color reminded Oliver of his collection of exotic butterflies—his hobbyhorse and quiet obsession.

Dazzling sapphire blues, glistening watermelon pinks, pulsating canary yellows with shimmering oranges—flew from the canvas, and ricocheted off the marble floor which had been polished to a mirror-like gleam.

He had commissioned the painting in a move of uncharacteristic impulsiveness eight years earlier when he was 22 and madly in lust with Ruby. A 20-year-old exotic beauty, she'd fluttered into his life, bringing with her eternal sunshine, and air so fresh it seeped through the iron fortress he'd built around his heart.

Butterfly Lovers encapsulated the vitality, optimism, and positivity she exuded. It was a rare piece which the serious art connoisseurs who gathered here this evening would die to possess. Oliver's brow furrowed, aware many were drawn here not by the desire to possess the contemporary art world's finest paintings, but insatiable voyeurs hungry to glimpse the inner world of one of America's wealthiest and most elusive bachelors.

Immensely private, he'd never opened any of his palatial homes to the public before. Not homes, *houses*, he corrected. He congratulated himself as he glanced around the clinical, museum-like surroundings. The dark walls and sophisticated lighting, spotlighting priceless works of art, created a sophisticated, yet austere, facade. If a building was truly a reflection of its owner, as many designers believed, the interior aptly reinforced the stereotypes perpetuated in the media—moody, dark, mysterious and strictly hands-off.

There was some truth to that, but it was not the whole truth.

Oliver's eyes drifted to the spiraling staircase and the heavy gold braided rope barricading the entrance to the upper level. He never let anyone get beyond the ground floor of his psyche. Some tried, but few persevered. No one, other than Ruby had ever penetrated his fortified armor. And that was a mistake.

He was complicated.

No doubt someone here tonight would go home and tweet that he was something of a social outcast, and arrogant to boot, Oliver thought as he hovered in the background. The fact was that he preferred his own company than engaging with his guests—predominantly wealthy financiers and bankers.

He knew his contempt was hypocritical, given he didn't care who reached into their pockets. But there was something decidedly unpalatable about bankers and the merciless way they preyed on the vulnerable. Tonight, he would gladly encourage them to part with their millions.

As he glanced at his reflection in the floorlength window it struck him how far he had come from the days when just finding money to support himself and his little sister had been a struggle. Resplendent in an immaculately tailored Dolce & Gabbana tuxedo cut from the finest Italian wool, he looked like he belonged.

Oliver rubbed his hand over his pecs, powerfully aware of the Maori-inspired tattoo coiled over his shoulder that the crisp white linen of his shirt concealed. His hands pulsed with renewed conviction. It was his touchstone—a symbolic reminder that he was fierce and untouchable—a warrior businessman and an impenetrable lover.

On a good day, he even fooled himself.

But no matter how easy it was to make millions, no matter how many things he acquired, he'd never found a sense of contentment.

Except with—

Oliver bit down on his teeth, grinding them together in a futile attempt to crush memories he was determined not to revisit.

He glanced at his Rolex. 7:03:02. Irritability coursed through his veins. What the hell was the auctioneer waiting for? He fixed him with a piercing look, firing his unspoken annoyance through the crowd.

Tardiness was something he abhorred, and doubly-so tonight, he thought as he locked on the important call he had to make. In one hour it would be 8am in New Zealand and his sister, as punctual as he was, would be anxiously waiting.

As though feeling the pointed tip of Oliver's anger the auctioneer looked up. His relaxed smile quickly shattered as he was forced to confront the aggressive glint in Oliver's eyes, the rigid set of his shoulders, the brutally hard line of his jaw.

The auctioneer banged his hardwood gavel on the sounding block with short urgent thuds, his florid face ballooning as the chatter continued.

"Ladies and gentlemen, can I have your attention?" More insistent hammering. "Attention! Attention!"

The chatter fell to an orderly whisper, extinguished finally by the auctioneer's solemn voice.

"As you know, tonight is a unique opportunity to savor the extraordinary passions of Oliver Hart. Renowned as an astute businessman, Oliver Hart is also an obsessive collector," he said.

"He has one of the most significant collations of contemporary art in the world. Not only a man of significant wealth, Oliver Hart, founder of Hart Luxury Hotel Consortium, is a man of outstanding generosity. All the funds raised by tonight's art auction will provide relief for those affected by last month's devastating earthquake in New Zealand, where he spent much of his childhood."

Oliver studied his feet as a thunder of applause quaked through the room, amplifying as it echoed off the walls.

Childhood.

The word was like a vicious punch to his stomach. Oppressive memories pounded his brain, and this time there was no silencing them.

Suddenly he was four years old again. Four years old and frightened. Lonely. Abandoned. Trapped in a jungle of strangers. Abandoned by bickering parents into a boarding school, neither one willing to let the other have custody. Selfishly caring more about winning against each other than the needs of their own child. And then there was his father.

His jaw locked as he bit down hard, swallowing a toxic cocktail of grief and anger. The brutal beatings hadn't hurt nearly as much as the verbal abuse and discouragement he'd suffered when he told them he wanted to be like his grandfather and study butterflies. The abuse had only intensified when he turned his back on the legal career his father had wanted. *'You'll never achieve anything. I wish you'd never been born. How dare you defy me you worthless piece of shit,'* the pain of these beatings had long healed—but those words still hurt.

Freezing sweat clung to Oliver's body in a vice-like grip, as he recalled the scorn his father rained upon him during his few personal visits. He paced across to the open window, inhaling deeply as he struggled to rip himself free from the shards of the past. Jesus, what sort of father tries to have his son institutionalized?

To some, it might seem ironic that he should be so generous to a country where he spent such an unhappy childhood, but Oliver didn't like to think of others suffering.

He forced his mind back to the present.

"Tonight's opening painting *Butterfly Lovers* is a significant artwork," the auctioneer continued, glancing down at his notes.

Oliver didn't have to read his words to know that what he would reveal was a shallow rendition of the truth. Only two people in the world truly knew just what *Butterfly Lovers* meant.

He glanced around the room thinking Ruby might have come, hoping with all his willpower she hadn't.

2

HE FORCED HIMSELF NOT TO BETRAY THE turmoil of emotions jack-knifing through his body as the massive painting was carried to the makeshift podium.

The butterfly theme had held so much promise. He'd never really bought into Ruby's tales about the transformative power of art to heal. But back then privately he'd hoped her optimism might rub off. With her by his side, and by owning the painting, perhaps he could shed a skin, free himself of his de-formed past, re-emerge in a new skin. Undamaged. Someone nearing perfection. A better man. The sort of man Ruby deserved.

He'd been a fool.

Oliver's spine stiffened. He'd intended to keep it

. . .

her . . . forever. But even good intentions couldn't make up for a lifetime's inability to commit. He moved towards the terrace, widening the distance between him and the painting. He would no longer succumb to the painting's potent power to remind him of his failings.

"Created specifically for Oliver over seven years ago by struggling contemporary artist CG Tombly— only Oliver could have foreseen its financial potential."

Oliver's brow furrowed. The suggestion he had acquired the painting for commercial gain, rankled him. If he wasn't such a private man he might have told the crowd the truth. He'd made the mistake of talking candidly once before—a mistake he wouldn't be making again.

In its place, he'd created a new habit—a habit of keeping his emotional life to himself, one he wasn't about to break. Soon the painting, and the painful memories of the only woman capable of making him feel, would be shed and he could devote himself to less painful obsessions.

"As always, Oliver's timing is impeccable. The painting's value has rocketed in the same soaring capacity as the palatial hotel Oliver's company has recently constructed in Dubai–so high it almost touches the gods."

The auctioneer flung his hands into the air to

accentuate his point. "Oliver Hart," he said, nodding in his direction and pointing to his towering 6-foot, 2-inch frame, "never does anything small."

Oliver thrust his hands in his pockets and glanced out the window refusing to look at the painting as the bidding began.

In a few fist-clenching minutes it would all be over and he could get on with his life.

His gaze drifted to the sculpture garden, lying beyond the pool, alighting on a solitary bronze sculpture by Brancusi. The modernist interpretation of Hercules holding the world on his shoulders, with its roughly hewn egg-shaped sphere symbolizing earth had always appealed to him.

Balanced precariously on a towering sculpted wood base, the odd shape and the large crater severing the middle of the sphere challenged conventional notions of perfection and reminded him of humanity's rawness.

As his gaze lingered over the sculpture it occurred to him that repairing his scars, so deep that no relationship he started ever endured, required a Herculean effort.

No wonder the painting had failed.

But he still wanted to believe, as the ancient Greeks had, that art had a powerful ability to transform lives. He only hoped that selling the painting finally fulfilled this purpose. Perhaps then the painful memories that still haunted him could be turned to good.

He turned and fixed his gaze upon the audience. Who would be its new owner he wondered as the opening bid of one million was made. Would it go to Don Hermes, the impotent pharmaceutical giant, standing just ahead of him, or some other equally innocuous purchaser? Or would some anonymous bidder calling from China, Europe or the Middle East be the lucky buyer?

"$12 million? Do I have $12 million?" The bags under the auctioneer's eyes shifted as he tilted his head forward, and peered under his glasses.

"A small price to pay," he continued, his gaze briefly flickering to Oliver, "for a painting personally commissioned by a man who defies every category and transcends every cliché: a man with tremendous gusto and creative generosity."

The auctioneer's eyes flew to a scantily dressed blonde hovering hopefully next to Oliver. "A man who has yet to be pinned down."

Oliver caste her a dismissive look and moved further toward the back of the room.

"$12 million we have," cried the auctioneer's assistant, nodding vigorously as he pressed his iPhone firmly to his ear.

Oliver's heart lurched as the bidding began.

"$13 million," the assistant taking telephone bids shouted, raising his hand.

"$13.2 million." The auctioneer's eyes darted between the phone bidder and two men determined to claim the painting as their own.

Explosive tension hovered as one of the two remaining bidders turned their attention away.

"$13.5 million! At $13.5 million the painting will be sold," the auctioneer warned. He suspended the gavel in the air, pausing as he scanned the room.

"$17.4 million," came a guttural, low growl from the front of the crowd.

A record price!

The room fell silent under the weight of the bid, then buzzed with irritatingly discordant voices, their murmurs of awe and envy a rising tide of white noise.

Oliver's eyes darted to the front row. Over $14 million? The price was ridiculous. Someone must want it desperately. But who and why?

He was acquainted with the deep pockets of unbridled obsession. He understood intimately the seductive power of the painting.

But this was crazy bidding.

There had to be a compelling reason surpassing the usual appreciation of any art-lover. At that price it could hardly be an investment buy.

So that left . . . what?

Oliver paced the back of the room in agitation unable to see the face of the man who had placed this latest bid. He caught a glimpse of the woman next to the anonymous bidder as she shook a sexy spill of sun-kissed curls down her back. The familiar gesture sent shockwaves to his heart.

It couldn't be.

Her head turned slightly.

Oliver stood still, as if turned to stone.

Ruby Diaz.

His Ruby.

3

A SYMPHONY OF EMOTIONS CRASHED through his veins as he saw a possessive arm snake around Ruby's waist and realized with horror the identity of the serpent she was with. Oliver threw back his shoulders, his muscular jaw tilted forward in defiance as he looked at the nauseatingly familiar figure.

Carlos Torres, the New York based, Mexican banking magnate and the-soon-to-be owner of *Butterfly Lovers.*

He could not let his painting—their painting—fall into her lover's clutches—a man as unscrupulous as he was deceptively charming.

Oliver's overactive mind raced with scenarios. He could draw from his own accounts the money for the earthquake fund—adding to the millions he had already donated.

But he knew with chilling certainty he was powerless to flout protocol, to bend the rules, to manipulate the outcome to suit his own desires. He knew only too well that once the auction had started, *Butterfly Lovers* could not be withdrawn.

"At this price, we'll sell," the auctioneer's eyes swept the room for any last bids.

The muscles in Oliver's chest tightened as he saw the auctioneer's gavel ascend into the air.

He watched helplessly as Carlos pulled Ruby toward him and folded her into his arms. The bitter taste of jealousy flooded his mouth.

The gavel sank toward the sounding block with freeze-frame inevitability. A splintering crack as wood met wood confirmed it was over with chilling clarity.

Oliver's hand tightened into a closed fist, crumpling the *Butterfly Lovers* catalog into obscurity.

His heart rate pulsated making his chest feel as though it was about to implode, as Ruby turned and he watched with shock the way she wilted under Carlos's dominant presence, the light of passion missing from her eyes. She seemed sad and vulnerable—and the Ruby he knew was neither.

Something was wrong.

His rational mind thundered a warning. Don't get involved.

What business was it of his if she wanted to make a life with that snake? None. Not ordinarily. But Ruby wasn't ordinary. Accepting and accommodating maybe, but something told him there was more to their union than met the eye.

He clenched his fists and cursed softly fighting against the impulse to save her from a big mistake. Playing rescuer would invite complications he didn't need.

Especially now.

What he needed was a distraction. What he needed was uncomplicated sex—not to reignite an obsession. Ruby had already proven herself capable of breaking his heart mercilessly.

Not so with paintings and sculptures and his beloved butterflies, he mused, forcing his thoughts back to his collections. Once possessed they would never leave without his consent. And he could never make them cry. His jaw clenched as bitter memories of his parents' feuding pounded in his ears. His mother's heart-wrenching cries once heard, never forgotten.

He must not be distracted. He must not allow Ruby to get close. Obviously she had engineered Carlos to buy the painting, knowing full well how it would torture Oliver. She tortured him all those years ago and it was clear she intended to continue the onslaught. She could have that damned painting, he mused as unwelcome, undesired, uncontrollable passions, long forgotten but now unbridled, threatened to escape.

He rested one shoulder against the panoramic window, his attention locked on Ruby as she freed herself from Carlos's clutches and fluttered through the swelling crowd toward the patio.

She possessed an innate and natural elegance that caused his glands to salivate, wetting his appetite in open defiance of his will. Her legs screamed danger—their long, slender length accented in scorchingly sharp stilettos that threatened to kill.

Kill his resolve. Kill his self-control. Kill him all over again.

He reached for a glass of whiskey from a passing waitress. He rocked the glass from side to side and studied the rough ice-chunks crashing through the amber liquid, then knocked the drink back, drowning his conflicting emotions.

Like a moth drawn to light he savored the way her floor-length, silk dress clung to her lithe figure, her hibiscus red dress shimmering under the halogen lights like the wings of a newly emerged butterfly.

The way the vibrant color of her dress contrasted so deliciously with the flock of black cocktail dresses and designer dark suits everyone else favored brought a smile to his lips. Ruby had always stood out from the crowd.

Walk away, stay away. The voice in his head pitched high and shrill like an ambulance siren, as he fought an instinctive need to free her from a bad mistake.

The irregularly cut crystal pressed into his fingers as he gripped the glass. His life had rapidly become complicated.

He craned his neck as he momentarily lost sight of her, searching over the sea of heads and glittering diamonds.

Like the shards of ice in his glass, his hardened intention to stay detached was fracturing.

Plastering on a face of extreme nonchalance, he pushed determinedly towards her through the crowd as she stepped onto the patio and gazed forlornly up at the stars.

Why the hell was she with a dickhead like Carlos.

Glancing at his watch, Oliver wondered if he could find out what he needed to know in less than 20 minutes?

MAGNETISM

Rivers of joy will follow attractions
to drop on the ring

~ Aniekee Tochukwu Ezekiel ~

4

CARLOS HAD BEEN DETERMINED TO purchase a work of art. He had demanded Ruby come. Instinctively every bone in her body wanted to refuse, but he had insisted. He hadn't mentioned the name of the artwork, and she hadn't asked why it was so crucial she be there.

'*Why?*' was not a question that either Carlos or her family condoned. The rules hadn't changed and the message was clear; *be a good girl and do what you're told.*

Ordinarily, she might have bitten back, but with her father so ill and her family facing financial ruin, now was not the time. They needed Carlos's money.

And Ruby always gave priority to other people's needs. The Diaz's had given her a home when nobody else wanted her. The only thing that mattered now was repaying their kindness.

But Carlos had played her like a fool. She swallowed her pride and the resentment of once again being used for other people's pleasure.

Her breath clung to her lungs as she walked toward the pool and filled her belly with deep gulps of the sweet fragrant air. There was no escaping her past.

Not now. Not here. Not in the home of the man she'd tried so hard to avoid.

Ruby turned around to make her way back to Carlos's side, knowing he would be furious if she was absent for long. Her mind was churning as a large muscular male blocked her path. She reached out her hand to avoid a collision.

A glittering frenzy of electrons surged through her body as her fingers connected with a crisp white shirt covering a far too muscular chest. Heat radiated through her in a wild, impulsive flood as firm hands gripped her upper arms.

Ruby froze. She didn't have to look up at the handsomely rugged face capping the majestically tall frame. Her body knew instinctively. Every muscle in her lithe frame quivered, the remembrance of their intimacy all those years ago permanently etched in her muscular memory bank.

Painting a smile onto quivering lips Ruby took a deep breath. For years she'd dreaded this moment.

"Hello Oliver," she said with just enough frost to make sure he knew she didn't care.

"You've been avoiding me," Oliver murmured in a deeply derisive voice.

Against common sense her gaze met his. She could tell from the gleam of hard ruthlessness which brought a sharper intensity to Oliver's eyes that he still blamed her for running out on him all those years ago.

But then he'd never understood the hold her family had over her. He'd never understood how much she strived for their approval. He'd never understood how they'd made her give up the only man she'd ever loved.

How could he know how deeply she'd grieved? She never told him. And now, after all this time, she doubted he cared. For some reason she never knew, family meant nothing to him.

He never talked about them. Not once.

Ruby willed herself to give away none of the turmoil coursing through her. She forced herself to study his far too ruggedly gorgeous face with veiled, unreadable eyes. She pressed her lips together, ensuring no excitement softened the mouth that had once possessed his in passionate, mindless enchantment.

"It's better we don't see each other Oliver," she said, feeling a tug of remorse, as the all too familiar heavy load of guilt squashed her heart. She wished she could tell him the truth, that everything he believed about her was a lie, but opening up and self-pity wasn't her style. Masking her insecurities with a cloak of aloofness was a much better defense, especially now.

Besides he'd hurt her too.

He left her emotionally well before she left him physically. She'd never forgiven him for abandoning her, preferring his aggressive pursuit of acquisitions and his relentless, and at times ruthless hunt for more and more wealth.

All to prove that he was worthy.

She'd been seduced by his commanding presence, his blatant masculinity, his overpowering protectiveness. In his arms she'd felt secure, adored, safe. Which was why his withdrawal came as such a shock.

Oliver was a lone wolf. A lone wolf she wasn't about to trust again with her heart. Even if her family would allow it. Which they wouldn't, she mused biting down on her lip.

Even if fate allowed—it was too late. The past was the past and revisiting it now would only make things worse. Carlos was their golden boy, the chains of connection locked in powerful family alliances.

He released his grip but stood firm. His eyes narrowed, his gaze unwavering. Music and laughter pulsated around them, but she was trapped with him in exploding silence.

Ruby felt a frisson of danger run down her spine as he towered over her. Not close enough for her to object but close enough to feel sparks ignite between them.

She stepped back, widening the space between them. She didn't want to feel what she felt. She *couldn't* feel what she felt. She *wouldn't* feel the magnetism that united them and branded her as his.

5

FOR YEARS SHE HAD NOT ALLOWED HERSELF to think of Oliver. She'd deleted all the photos of him from her hard drive, disciplined herself not to Google his name or surf the Internet for images, knowing that the only way to forget him was to try and erase his memory.

But that wasn't easily done. The papers were always full of his successes—both in business and in bed. Clearly, she had never been good enough. Not that it mattered now.

"I don't want to see you." She paused for extra effect, needing to rock his arrogant, determined, unflinching bravado. "I'm with someone else."

A gleam of hard ruthlessness brought a sharper intensity to his eyes, and Ruby felt pinned by him.

"So I see. What's the attraction?"

"It's called commitment, Oliver—something you wouldn't know about."

His piercing green eyes narrowed, then rested for long, uneasy moments on Ruby's quivering lips. His gaze moved with leisurely thoroughness before dropping to where the silk of her dress clung to her breasts.

His gaze, although openly sexual, was a naked, stark claim. "What we've got is an inconvenient response to each other. Eight years hasn't diluted that."

A frightening sexual heat, the remnant of a time when the slightest look, the merest scrap of attention from this man had whipped her body into tumultuous whirlpools of passion, battled with fury and pride.

Ruby's hands flew to her hips, "It's not inconvenient, untimely, or inopportune. It's unwanted. You're unwanted."

His smile hardened. He flinched as though she was a dentist and her words a drill striking a buried nerve.

"I see you've moved on," he said, tossing a dismissive look in Carlos's direction.

Ruby fixed her gaze on the marble floor. "Carlos and I are happy." The words limped from her mouth like a damp whisper.

"Why don't I believe you?" Oliver lifted her chin. His eyes engaged hers with intoxicating intensity. "I know you, Ruby. You can't lie to yourself. Not for long. *Not without suffering.*"

Her heart was thudding so loudly she felt certain he must be able to hear. If she were not so proud she would tell him that her family had all but lost their fortune, that Carlos had generously bailed them out of debt, that he asked for nothing but, when he felt the time was right, her hand in marriage.

She had managed to delay the inevitable but not for much longer. Yes, if she was not so stubbornly proud and loyal to the Diaz's she would put him out of his misery.

But she owed him nothing. Besides if he'd cared he would have chased after her. But he hadn't and she didn't trust the sudden attention.

She looked directly at him, sweeping a tendril of curling hair from her face, then smoothing her evening gown with trembling hands.

"Bold and as attractive as you are, you're also a fool. A fool to think you can push your way back into my life. A fool for thinking I still care." Ruby didn't enjoy being so cruel, but she had to push him away. Forever. Too much was at stake.

Oliver grabbed her hand and pulled her toward

him. "No man can make you lose yourself like I can."

Ruby followed his gaze as it drifted toward Carlos, eyes narrowing like a marksman.

"You're jealous. That's what this is all about. You don't care a damn about me. All you care about, all you've ever cared about is winning, beating, conquering. I'm not a trophy Oliver Hart. And I'm not yours to win."

"Forget him," his voice quaked with an urgency that surprised and frightened her. Impulsively he grabbed her hand, shocking her anew by the electric contact of his strong fingers encasing hers.

"Forget him," he repeated, gesturing to Carlos who had stopped to talk to a woman painted into a black sequined dress. The raw, forceful note in his voice demanded compliance.

Ruby met his gaze in an open challenge. "I can't," she rasped, tearing her arm free. She would not be a target for his wanton pleasure, waiting for him to mark her as his own, waiting for him to claim her, then freeze her out again.

Not now. Not tomorrow. Not ever. Not again. She'd been there, got the "I Fell for Oliver Hart tee-shirt" and it still hurt.

Something about the way he looked at her warned that he was a man on a quest and would not rest until he'd won. His eyes blazed dangerously, gleaming like the crystals that hung in the Murano glass chandeliers above. One wrong move and everything her family was fighting for could come crashing down she mused as she lifted her gaze to the ceiling.

She felt herself flinch involuntarily as Carlos drew alongside her wrapped his arms around her like a man protecting his most prized possession. Other women found him attractive, why couldn't she?

"She's a beautiful piece, Oliver," Carlos said, thrusting his hand forward.

She watched Oliver for his reaction, but he barely registered Carlos's arrival. His gaze hardened as he locked on her clenched fists, then rose to her eyes, his brow furrowed.

He knows.

She forced herself to fold into Carlos's rigid embrace fearful of his obsession with protecting the vulnerable. She was not vulnerable. She did not need rescuing.

Not by him.

"How could you stand to part with her?" Carlos continued with a smug look as Oliver gripped his outstretched hand.

The two men stared at each other like opposing gridiron players, their shoulders tense, muscles rippling.

"We were catching up on the past," she said throwing cold water on the mounting tension.

"A very passionate past," Oliver added, ignoring Ruby's dark look of warning.

She sensed Oliver wanted to smudge the self-satisfied smile off Carlos's face. Instead, he pulled his hand free, ran his fingers through his tousled licorice hair, swept an unruly wave across the back of his head, and straightened his black silk bow tie.

"I'm glad to see the painting did so well," he said, ignoring Carlos's thinly disguised reference to Ruby.

Carlos's brow furrowed momentarily before a politician's smile kicked into gear. "Who would have thought you and I would share a passion." His free arm coiled around Ruby's waist and pulled her towards him.

Oliver smiled sardonically. "So it would seem; a passion for rare and beautiful objects." He stared at Ruby with unswerving intensity, noticing with not a small degree of satisfaction the slight crimson tinge flushing her cheeks. "I'm referring of course to *Butterfly Lovers*," he said, his lips twisting as he turned to Carlos. "Congratulations on your purchase."

Carlos grunted.

"Nothing beats setting your sights on something beautiful and going after it. Nothing beats finding something you thought you'd never know. And nothing beats getting something others covet," Oliver said, his voice heavy with intent.

Carlos's chest swelled like a primal ape ready to charge. "I quite agree. You know I've just thought of the perfect spot for my painting. I think I'll hang it over our bed."

Carlos bared his teeth in what was known in business circles as his cobra smile "Now if you'll excuse us, all this talk of my success has made me ravenous."

"U NBELIEVABLE." RUBY SHOOK HER HEAD, sending a spill of sexy curls tumbling down her back. "I'm sorry, am I keeping you from something?" she said caustically, as Oliver glanced at his watch.

Oliver's stomach churned, both at her annoyance with him and the thought of *Butterfly Lovers* and Ruby entombed in Carlos's life like some Napoleonic conquest. Did she have any idea how repugnant the thought of his painting hanging over their bed was? He felt sick.

He glanced at his watch again. 7:55. He really wanted to sort this out but the only thing that was important right now was his sister Jacqui who was anxiously waiting for his call.

"You know there's nothing lonelier than being with a man who is always thinking about business and wishing he was somewhere else. I can't believe it, even after all this time—"

Oliver didn't bother arguing. Didn't she realize that all those years they'd been together that he'd spent aggressively pursuing property and amassing extraordinary wealth it was for her? He didn't bother explaining that when he'd dropped her home after a date that he'd been on the cusp of proposing and overheard her parents saying he would never amount to anything.

Instead, he vowed to prove them wrong—that he wasn't common, that he wasn't Kiwi trash, that he would make something of his life and provide for their daughter. He wanted to say, 'Ruby, don't you realize that all those hours I put into work were so we would never be apart?' But he said nothing. What was the point—he wasn't going to pursue a relationship with her and risk another heartbreak.

He shrugged. "What can I say?"

She looked at him, her sexy mouth pressed into a grim line, and shook her head. "Unbelievable."

It irked him that Ruby thought so little of him, especially now when making money and the shallow pursuit of wealth was the furthest thing from his mind. Besides, he'd worked his butt off to build his empire. Not like Carlos who inherited everything he owned.

Trying to explain what was preoccupying his thoughts now wasn't an option. His sister had sworn him to secrecy and while Oliver Hart may be accused of many things he never broke a confidence.

Oliver watched the back of Ruby's head as she stormed off, then he strode across the marble floor toward the stairs. He gripped the gold-braided barrier and flung it roughly to one side.

Let her believe the worst. If she hated him fine. What did he care? He bit back the metallic taste of bile lapping his gut, calling him a liar.

An unwelcome image of Ruby floated before his eyes. Pure as sunlight. Rare as a yellow diamond. Skin luminous as a pearl. His heart swelled momentarily as he thought of her. His gaze narrowed, his teeth clenched in steely determination as he dislodged her from his mind.

The only thing that was important was the butterfly. His sister Jacqui, a doctor, had explained to him at length how the meconium ejected by the butterfly as it left its chrysalis could produce the antibodies which could fight the rare wasting disease which threatened her life.

All he'd heard was the words 'possible miracle cure'. Right now, a miracle was the only thing that could save Jacqui. And she was all he had left.

With long, muscular legs he leaped up the stairs, three at a time. Ruby's animosity made it all the easier to keep dangerous feelings firmly locked away. He'd be damned if she'd control him again.

His mind floated to his quest—the pursuit of the rare papilionoidae species, unique to Oaxaca in Mexico and said to look like a flying gold pearl. Oliver renamed it the Hope butterfly—an apt description given the heights of hope that both he and his sister had pinned on it.

He ran his hand round his far too constricting collar, then loosened his top button, finally freeing himself of the tie around his neck—an unwelcome reminder of a lifestyle he disdained.

Oliver strode toward his bedroom and opened the door. Tension drifted away as he shut the extroverted world firmly out. He was allergic to clutter and incessant noise. Just one of many occupational, lifestyle hazards he had to endure, and one he had hoped to escape when he flew to Mexico in the morning.

He took in the uncluttered minimalist interior before striding over to his triple king size bed and picked up his black encased iPhone from the bedside table. He looked at the screen. 7:59. It seemed like an eternity as he waited the extra minute to call her as scheduled.

His thoughts locked on his younger sister Jacqui. Only eleven months separated them. Despite the fact they'd gone to separate boarding schools, Jacqui knew him better than anyone. How any parent could separate their children let alone shove two four-year-old kids in boarding schools in the name of love escaped them both. Maybe that was why they both clung so fiercely to their independence.

And to each other.

Oliver punched in the numbers, pushing down repressed feelings with each digit he pressed.

Finally, he had the opportunity to do something truly worthy. Far more worthy than amassing a monopoly board of towering hotels and mindless beauties.

"She's within range," he said hearing Jacqui's familiar Kiwi accent. "I reckon this time I'll get her." Oliver's normally measured voice pulsated with excitement. Pride, satisfaction, and fulfillment lifted the corners of his mouth.

"You've been searching for that butterfly for the past few months. What makes you think you're going to succeed now?" Jacqui said, her tone cautious.

Oliver hesitated. Had he spoken too prematurely? Had he given his sister false hope? "One of the guys on the butterfly forum unintentionally posted the missing part of the puzzle. For the first time I've found its breeding ground."

"That's fantastic, but why do I get the feeling something's wrong? You sound tentative."

"It only flies for one week." He said deliberately holding back the other obstacle he had yet to face. *Ruby*.

"Tight odds, but if anyone can do it you can."

Oliver laughed. 'Yeah, Indiana Jones of the butterfly world. That's me.'

"Oh, Oliver. I can't believe it," Jacqui said, her normally measured voice trembling, "the news couldn't come at a better time."

Oliver's attention snapped back to the moment. Panic pulsed through his veins. "What's wrong?"

The phone went silent.

"Jacqui, it's *me* you're talking to. Your brother— not one of your medical fraternity you can't talk to honestly. Spill!" Oliver pressed.

"The tremors in my hands—" Her voice trembled. "Oh Oliver, if this gets worse my surgical career will be ruined."

"The meconium—you said it would provide the cure."

"Yes, but only if we can get source it before it is too late."

"Too late?" Oliver fought to keep his voice from betraying the fear that raked his chest. "We're not giving up." His sister, a renowned pediatric surgeon, had fought overwhelming obstacles to claw her way to the top. She'd worked three jobs, tutored disadvantaged kids at night, and still managed to ace her exams, only to spend most of her working life battling the predominantly male profession. On hard-fought-for merit she was given an equal opportunity to excel only to find her efforts sabotaged by men who found her threatening.

Oliver slammed his open palm against the wall. He would not let a rare degenerative disease rob his little sister of everything she'd worked for. And he would not let it rob his sister of her life.

"The meconium—tell me how it works again."

"As the butterfly leaves the chrysalis it ejects meconium, the red fluid—"

Oliver's mouth curved into a rare smile. "You're talking to the butterfly man, I know what meconium is, Sis. But why this butterfly?"

"Pharmaceutical cures are making large companies zillions of dollars all the time failing my clients and others like them all around the world. The only good they've done is provide short-term relief and create legalized drug addicts. I've spent years researching natural cures for my clients. Do you remember Granddad's journals?"

Oliver nodded. Fred Hart had been a world-renowned naturalist and acclaimed researcher.

Oliver had never understood why when his grandfather had died he'd left his butterfly collection to Oliver and his journals to Oliver's sister. But as Jacqui told him of the pioneering research she had discovered, research that pointed unquestionably to the Hope butterfly, he knew it was fated.

His sister was destined to find a cure for the debilitating disease that threatened her and Oliver would capture the magical ingredient. Their destinies had always been entwined.

Oliver didn't need his sister to provide further fuel to embark on his quest. There was nothing he wouldn't do to help her, even if it involved less than conventional approaches to finding a cure for the debilitating wasting disease that stalked her like an oppressive shadow.

"No one can ever know, Oliver. *Nobody*," she emphasized. "The medical world is deeply traditional, suspicious of anything that isn't crushed into a pill. If it gets out, they'll think I'm a quack, a white-witch tinkering with voodoo magic. But if the antibodies in the meconium work like I think it will be a miracle cure—one the pharmaceutical giants will stop at nothing to suppress."

Her voice, deadly serious, had dropped to a whisper. "I'm not ill enough yet to be worried—but Oliver, if they suspect I may be dying they'll oust me from my role. I can't lose my job. It would kill me."

Oliver pressed his lips into a grim line. He knew full well the agony his sister suffered. Without their work to distract them they had nothing but bitter, lonely lives. Work gave them purpose. A reason to live.

"I won't let you down. It will be our secret," he said, masking the full force of his contempt for the industry his sister could not turn to in need.

As Oliver ended the call he stretched out on his bed and stared up at the sketch Picasso had drawn of his lover, an artist named Fernardo, which hung above his contemporary padded headboard. She was Picasso's first long term relationship—the woman he loved with such a passion he infuriated her with his zealous attempts to claim her as his own.

For one reckless, dangerous, illicit moment his thoughts coiled toward Ruby. He pillowed his head on his hands and closed his eyes. Butterflies were his passion, but she had once been the great love of his life. Was life giving him a second chance at love?

Nope, stupid, reckless, dangerous, he growled inwardly, startled by the weakness of his resolve. Hadn't he learned his lesson? A broken heart, a vulnerable heart, a traitorous heart left you vulnerable to attack.

Suddenly his bedroom door flew open. Ruby

walked in looking every inch as delicious as the woman in the painting.

"I'm sorry, I was looking for the bathroom." She stood stiffly like a sculpture, her posture frozen in suspended conflict as though weighing up whether to flee or stay. Her body might be rigid but her eyes widened, glistening illicitly like the iridescent scales of the giant swallow-tailed butterfly he hoped to find, as her gaze lingered on his virile body sprawled upon the bed.

Oliver bolted upright. He didn't buy her story about looking for the bathroom, but against his will, his heart stirred as he honed in on her achingly familiar curls and lithe body.

What the hell was he going to do? How much had she overheard? The breeding ground of the butterfly that could save his sister's life surrounded her family land in Mexico. What if she asked him to explain his conversation?

He couldn't tell Ruby why he needed to go to Mexico. His sister had sworn him to secrecy. Besides, Ruby had already proven herself capable of betraying his trust. Who was to say, she wouldn't do it again?

And he couldn't tell Jacqui that the woman who had mutilated his heart so mercilessly had reappeared—she'd only question her sworn bachelor-brother relentlessly.

But he couldn't leave Ruby in the hands of Carlos either.

His greatest strength was also his greatest flaw. *Loyalty*. Whatever he did he knew he had to protect both women. The question was, how?

PASSION

There is only one passion,
the passion for happiness

~ Denis Diderot ~

7

HEAT FLAMED RUBY'S BODY AS SHE TORE HER eyes away from Oliver spread-eagled across the bed. Was she mistaken or was he being deliberatively provocative?

She tried to ignore the sensual turbulence threatening her equilibrium as Oliver's eyes all but undressed her.

It was a purely male assessment, appreciative and primally charged. To Ruby's intense chagrin her body responded with wild urgency forcing her body to rigid attention.

Ruby dragged her mind to Carlos; the man her family were determined she would spend the rest of her life with. Carlos was a skilled politician—diplomatic when he needed to be and not afraid to commit—the complete opposite of Oliver.

But to her intense discomfort, she found herself wishing Carlos didn't make her freeze every time he touched her.

She jumped as something furry curled its way around her legs. "You have a cat?" she said with surprise, bending down and trailing her fingers along the velvety black fur.

His voice was slightly mocking. "A pair."

"Two cats?"

"People own cats you know."

"People, yes—but not you."

Only affectionate people have cats.

Or damaged ones, she mused, noticing how her heart kicked at the unexpected realization that Oliver might understand, as she did, the power of an animal's unconditional love to heal.

"Renshaw and Edwards. A boy and a girl."

"What strange names? Are they famous?"

"Yes—but not for the right things. They were a couple of high profile lawyers in New Zealand who fleeced their clients of millions. The cats remind me never to let down my guard. And I like that they don't demand anything from me."

Oliver clicked his long manicured fingers and another black cat ran toward him and leaped onto the bed. It coiled around Oliver, purring loudly. He picked it up and ruffled his fingertips under its chin.

For a shocking moment Ruby imagined herself coiled around his legs too, her face nuzzled against his chest, feeling protected and adored. Heat flamed her face.

The devil danced in his eyes as he grinned. If she were a mind-reader she'd swear he'd mistaken her thoughts and was assessing whether she'd purr like a contended pussy or would she roar like an untamed lion as he claimed her and demonstrated his sexual virility.

Her stomach cramped with nervous tension.

"You're still a beautiful woman, Ruby."

Ruby responded with a dismissively blank expression. Inwardly his compliment made her heart dance a happy jig. What was she thinking? He was seducing her and she needed to get out of his lair fast before he succeeded.

Something mischievous and far too dangerous danced in Oliver's eyes as she turned to leave. He rose from the bed and strode toward her. She hesitated, suspended in one aching moment between desire and fear.

"How long were you outside my door?"

"Not long," she told him. Her body jittered with the half-truth. 'Why?' She wanted to ask, 'Why did you say I was nearly within reach? Who were you boasting to that this time you'd get me?' But she said nothing.

Something shuttered down over his eyes. He was silent for a moment. "I want to show you something."

"What?" she rasped.

His lips curved into a sensuous smile. "My passion."

"I can't. I won't," she whispered, her breath crawling the arch of her lungs. She dragged her gaze from him and scanned the room, her gaze locked on the sexually provocative portrait hanging over his bed. Why in God's name was she standing there? It was lunacy. She tried to ignore the sensual turbulence threatening her equilibrium.

"Butterflies."

"Butterflies?" Ruby's heart ached inexplicably. She should have felt relieved. Confusion rose to meet intrigue. Why on earth would a testosterone-laden, alpha male like Oliver be interested in something so fragile and beautiful?

His breath fanned the top of her head as he towered over her. "I'd like to show you my private collection. Unless of course, you're afraid of being alone with me?" Oliver said, knowing full well the power of his challenge.

Keeping the smile pinned on, Ruby looked directly at him. "Why would I be afraid of you?" her normally calm voice quivered.

"Perhaps you have to ask Carlos's permission?" Oliver said, his voice richly marinated in sarcasm.

She threw him a mocking glance. "Jerk," she muttered under her breath. She didn't know what riled her more, Oliver's power to arouse her, or her inability to say no to his request.

Being with him was dancing with danger. But there was something hypnotic about the way he looked at her, as though he was a bee, and she a flower, blossoming under the intensity of his dangerous unpredictability, feeling as though for the first time a light had been turned on.

To her excruciating chagrin she desired the exciting, dangerous, extreme sexual chemistry that sizzled between them. Until this evening she had forgotten a man could affect her as Oliver always had.

He was obviously toying with her. Well, he would find himself evenly matched, she vowed.

A thrill of rebelliousness danced through her veins as an arrogant smile tilted his lips, giving his mouth a subtle sensuality that morphed into unashamed desire. She cautioned herself against playing with fire—afraid of what might happen next.

A slight blush heated her cheeks as Oliver

studied her with unswerving intensity. Ruby was physically conscious of herself more than she had ever been in her life: conscious of the silk of her dress caressing her thighs; conscious of the diamond necklace nestled between her quivering breasts; conscious of the dryness of her throat as she swallowed a melody of stirring emotions.

And she knew her blue eyes were no longer clear ponds of still water. They were hot and bothered with the awakening of explosive passions. Passions he'd heartlessly said she didn't possess when they were together years ago.

His smoldering eyes tormented and enticed her as he paused at a door at the end of the hall and punched in a code. As the door sprung open, a wave of hot, dry air engulfed her.

It was crazy. She should be getting the hell out of there. But she couldn't help herself.

Could he feel the butterflies that danced in her stomach as she entered his private sanctuary? His eyes were still on her face, reminding her of a wild panther, watching, waiting for the right moment to pounce.

She wondered, too late, if playing with a renowned seducer like Oliver Hart wasn't 50 shades too dangerous?

8

WHAT MADE HER DO IT, SHE DIDN'T KNOW.

Nor did she stop to assess the danger as she left the safety of the hallway and entered what was clearly a secret, highly revered room.

Curiosity had claimed her. Not even an uneasy sense of disloyalty to Carlos acted as a deterrent. Oliver was drawing a heated reaction from her that set every nerve in her body vibrating with exultant, primitive life, and only once in her twenty-eight years had she felt anything like it before

Her whole body tingled with an electric awareness as he stood beside her. She wanted to look at his face, wanted to see if the desire was still in Oliver's eyes—but she no longer dared.

He was too close, too dangerously close if she

was to keep some semblance of control. She had been insanely mad to come to him. Sanity insisted that she give him no more encouragement.

Far better, she thought, to fixate on the beauty of the butterflies in his collection than succumb to the passions Oliver's close presence incited.

Her eyes flew to the handcrafted cabinets that lined the walls of the carefully air-conditioned room.

His richly tanned hands gently slid back the doors of one of the floor-to-ceiling cabinets lining the room. Strong hands, with long, supple fingers curled around the edges of an ebony rimmed tray, topped with glass.

With the care of a parent picking up his baby from its crib, Oliver lifted the tray and placed it on a highly polished antique Chinese desk. A heady scent of beeswax and Camphor crystals filled the room as he lifted the protective glass.

Ruby stood absolutely still, her gaze determinedly fixed on the most dazzlingly beautiful kaleidoscope of butterflies she had ever seen.

Color exploded around her, sending earthly thoughts scrambling. Shots of lipstick pink morphed into purples and trailed out to rich raw umber browns. Lustrous blues, tinged with effervescent orange-reds jostled for attention with dazzling emerald greens, splashed with electric violets, charming her eyes with their captivating colors.

Whether it was Oliver's presence and the sizzling chemistry that sparked between them, the sensual scent of beeswax, or the hypnotic effect of the dazzling butterflies Ruby didn't know. But she felt short of breath, her heart rate quickening as her hungry eyes devoured the pulsating chocolate box of colors.

Oliver's powerful chest swelled as though clearly relishing in her visceral reaction. "Flying flowers," he whispered in reverence to their beauty.

"They're exquisite," Ruby murmured. She leaned closer until her face almost touched the glass.

"You won't find any rips or tears or smudges in my collection," he said. "I source my butterflies like people buy diamonds. I demand perfection."

Insecurity snaked through Ruby's mind. Thank God she'd worn her Spandex. She was not the unblemished young girl he once knew. Her body, with its little pockets of cellulite, would never live up to his exacting standards. She pushed the thought from her mind. Besides, it wasn't as if he'd ever see her naked.

Again.

She ignored the worming feeling of regret that

coiled through her gut and turned her attention back to the safety of his collection.

Ruby watched mesmerized as the man with the athletic build of a gridiron player and the swagger of a rodeo cowboy lifted one of nature's most delicate creations with the micro-skills of New York's finest surgeons.

"Human tissue mends but butterflies don't," he said.

Ruby wanted to tell him he was wrong. Hearts don't mend, but she thought better of sharing her feelings.

"Their scales are as thin as tissue paper and as breakable as filo pastry left in the sun."

He held an iridescent beauty up to the light. Like patterns on a soap bubble, the colors shimmered and varied with the changing angle of view.

"You're looking at the startling and intense iridescent Blue Morphos from the Amazon." His gaze shifted from the butterfly to Ruby. "Startling because its color is so incredibly rich and deep. Foil-like and utterly gorgeous," he hesitated, then looked directly at her. "Just like your eyes."

Ruby blamed the confines of the room for the hot flush that rose to her cheeks. He *was* playing with her. She wrenched her eyes away from his cool, steady stare.

"How many butterflies do you own?" she asked, flitting to a safer topic.

"A few thousand. Give or take a hundred."

"Gosh, I never knew there were so many different kinds? Where on earth did you find them?"

He paused, as though deciding how much he should confide. "I inherited the collection from my grandfather. He was a renowned researcher and collector—as was his father before him. They discovered species new to science and documented these in scientific papers. Grandad's only regret," he said, his gaze lingering on a butterfly set apart from the others, "was that he never discovered the female of this species—thus making it a pair. That would have been quite a feat—she is so very rare."

His voice dropped to a whisper as though he was confiding a secret. "Personally I love the butterflies freedom and seeing them in the wild makes my heart soar, but I also value the legacy that collections such as these leave. The only request my grandfather made was that I agree to be their guardians. When I pass—" his tone became somber, unsettling her. "—when I die, should I have no heir, it is to be gifted to the Natural History Museum. It's a fitting way to preserve both the butterflies and my grandfather's memory."

For a traitorous moment Ruby's heart kicked. It wasn't supposed to be like *this*, so all-consuming.

Her deepening admiration for the way he cared for his grandfather, the softness in his tone and touch as he appreciated the butterflies' delicate beauty, the intimacy he was showing her now by allowing her into his inner sanctuary. Guilt twisted with longing in a sharp rivet of pain from her gut to her chest.

She wished she would be the woman to bear him an heir.

How could she feel this rush of longing? It had been eight years . . . she was with Carlos now. She had assured herself that after all this time she no longer had feelings for Oliver. Yet she felt herself hover on the edge of control. She pushed the reckless thought out of her mind, as far as she could while he produced another tray of butterflies. What she needed was a distraction.

They were so heavenly, so gorgeous, so pretty. It didn't surprise her that he should fall under their spell. As she watched Oliver's eyes glisten with joy, it fascinated and unnerved her that these delicate beauties could reduce this hard muscular man to near tears and induce such feverish delight. It was a contagious joy that was as exciting as it was unsettling.

"You can never have enough passion," she said. God only knew why she of all people should utter such dangerous, reckless words. The unspoken desire pulsated between them.

Ruby's heart thundered a warning as passion oozed through the confined space.

Be careful.

As Oliver withdrew more trays for her pleasure caution reminded her that a man who could be caught in such an obsession could not be taken lightly.

His face was close enough for her to see the lines of ruthless purpose stamped on them. When she glanced into his eyes they were the eyes of a man who could take forceful possession of anything he wanted.

He crossed the room too quickly for her to register his intent. His hand reached out and took her arm. Surprise rendered her immobile as he pinned her to the wall.

She coolly met his eyes, suppressing a wild desire that he would seize a kiss. There was no mistaking the undiluted lust burning in those glistening, brilliant eyes.

Oliver was amoral, selfish, a rogue who meant to take whatever he desired, and he meant to take it tonight.

Loyalty slammed an invisible steel wall between them saving her from doing something she would live to regret.

"I can't," Ruby said, turning her face away as Oliver attempted to steal a kiss.

"Can't or won't?" his raspy voice penetrated every fiber of her being.

"Both," she said, biting back the urge for once in her life to forget being the good girl.

"When are you going to stop fighting what you feel?"

"Feel what?" Ruby closed her eyes, willing herself to stay strong.

"How it is between us. How it's always been. Is it a crime to still want you?"

He curled long perfectly manicured fingers around the soft part of her forearm, gently holding her captive. "All I want to do is kiss you—nothing immoral."

He pressed her firmly against the wall. She felt pinned, captured, imprisoned for Oliver's perverse pleasure—just like the butterflies she'd been admiring.

She knew better than anyone it would not stop at a kiss. He would take her beyond her boundaries of control. She felt drunk with the depth of his desire. Giddy, light-headed, reckless.

But Ruby wasn't reckless. She was trustworthy, she was someone others relied on, someone who always put everyone's needs before her own. She was not someone who would act impulsively. And she wouldn't, couldn't, mustn't let her family down.

She twisted and pulled away—severing the invisible ties that bound them together.

Oliver's eyes darkened. "What are you afraid of Ruby? Me or the depths of your desire?"

Ruby folded her arms and pressed them across her chest. "I'm not afraid of you. I'm not afraid of anything," she retorted angrily.

"I know you. Perhaps better than you know yourself. You can't live without passion."

"Carlos and I have passion," she lied.

"Okay then." Oliver lifted his arms in surrender. "Fly away then Ruby, back to the one who fills your body, your soul, your heart with fire."

Ruby hesitated, frustratingly unable to get her legs to do her bidding. Oliver was right, there was no fire. There was no passion. There was no love. What Carlos and she had was pragmatism, under-standing, convenience.

But she would not be the one to reveal the truth. Passion, she'd been warned was a fatal, dangerous thing like a wild horse that could tear your heart and run away with your sanity.

If passion was so wrong why did she feel drowned by an overwhelming wave of regret as she fought to distance herself from him?

A defiant, knowing smirk consumed Oliver's devilishly handsome face, igniting an inner deter-mination to break free from the suffocating room, and the reach of his illicit magnetism.

9

O LIVER WASN'T SURE WHAT PROMPTED HIM.

He wasn't foolish enough to dance with danger. He hadn't intended to take things this far. Normally his emotions were tightly controlled. But as he gazed into Ruby's face instinct took over. He touched his tongue to his lips, narrowed his eyes, moved toward her, one thing in mind.

Her eyes widened and her soft, sensuous lips parted, staring at his mouth with uncertainty. A soft salmon blush settled upon her cheeks. Ruby's body moved toward him involuntarily. Desirous, yearning, needy.

"I must go," she said thickly, as though forcing herself to fight the physical magnetism he was exerting.

He leaned toward her. "You can't help what you feel," Oliver murmured in his low, seductive voice. "You want to taste me as much as I want to taste you."

His face came closer, his eyes commanding hers with relentless purpose.

"Oliver . . . I . . . I can't," she stammered, pushing him gently as he approached.

His eyes narrowed sensuously as his gaze lingered on her throat, on her heaving breasts, on her trembling body, filled with passion—and with promise.

Ruby shrunk back, hard against the wall. He lifted an arm, placing his palm firmly on the wall near her ear.

"I've missed you," he whispered, bringing his lips to within centimeters of hers.

He could feel the electrical charge that unified and ignited their bodies. He could hear the quickening gasps of breath.

He inhaled her familiar scent, savoring memories of the steamy sex they'd once enjoyed. Eight years later he could still smell her sweet musky essence after that night of lovemaking. He could still hear her moans of pleasure. He could still feel her body tense as ecstasy sent ripples through her body.

He wanted to turn back the hands of destiny, to reclaim the time lost to them. One minute he was leaning toward her, and the next he was lost in a tropical utopian dream. Soft, sensual, vibrant, surrounded by fragrant breezes and the feel of the warm earth beneath his bare feet.

Ruby let out a breathy sigh just before his lips touched hers. So softly, so gently, he wasn't sure if it was real. He felt her body stiffen, then tremble as she folded into him.

He moaned as Ruby's slender arms draped around his neck. His mouth sought hers with a slow deliberation that eased the throb of need deep within him. Gently he took her top lip in his mouth and softly sucked it, slowly savoring her taste. He opened his mouth to drink more of her intoxicating elixir. She opened for him, tasting of honey and paradise.

With a touch like a butterfly, he kissed her eyelids, then softly brushed her cheeks with his lips. He held her neck gently in his hands, caressed the tips of her earlobes with his lips, blew soft kisses in her ear.

Ruby's whole being vibrated in wild response to his. He sensed she was utterly helpless to stop him from doing anything he wanted with her.

His hands slid under her silky dress, stroking the smooth skin of her back. He pressed her closer until he felt the pounding beat of her heart against his chest.

The sounds of the music rising, rhythmic humming and people chattering as they partied below could barely be heard over the roar of longing in his heart.

They remained close as though frozen in a moment. He closed his eyes and marveled at how wonderful it was to be with her again. Her kisses quenched his thirst, watered the dry, barren, parched wasteland of his life.

Her sensual touch provided a welcome tonic for the boring monotony of soulless encounters.

He felt the flutter of the cool air on his face, streaming through the vents, heard the faint sound of a musician, acoustic guitar in hand, strumming songs of love. And lost himself in mindless enchantment. Then, he felt a shove to his chest.

"Stealing a kiss may not be immoral in your mind, but you and I both know you don't give a damn about who you hurt, or whose life you ruin," she said, projecting the guilt and anger she felt at her own weakness onto him, as she opened the door and fled.

"You can't lie to yourself, not for long," he said, his voice a dark prophecy, chasing after her as she fled.

"Forget it. Forget me. Forget us," she cried.

10

H E SHOULDN'T CARE, BUT HE DID. HE couldn't put his finger on what was troubling him more—his success in deliberately frightening her away or his annoyance that she had fled to Carlos.

His hand trembled uncharacteristically as he lifted the remaining tray of butterflies and slid it back in the cabinet. Oliver gritted his teeth and shook his head at his weakness.

He shouldn't be getting involved. He was a tough man, a ruthless man, a man not easily swayed. A man who should have better control over his emotions. But a man, nevertheless. A man hard-wired with carnal feelings and lusting for the feminine form, intrinsically drawn to the opposite flesh.

But Ruby was so right, he didn't do commitment. He'd seen his father's commitment to his mother turn into obsessive control and vowed never to be like him—a man who loved so much he hurt those who captured his heart.

He turned to leave the room, sweeping his hands along the smooth surface of the cabinets, brushing aside the irony. Oliver knew he was being hypocritical but something about Ruby's pending loss of freedom to Carlos compelled a deep desire to protect her, possess her, make her his own.

But he knew it would be her downfall.

The first thing he did when he saw a beautiful specimen of Lepidoptera was to curtail its freedom. But he knew that in doing so he was also protecting them from the ravages of the wasps and other predators who preyed on their beauty and innocence.

His mind drifted back to Ruby. He knew with punching clarity that the only way for Ruby to live as she deserved, was to free her. Free her from the clutches of her manipulative, controlling family, and free her from the man he knew with gut-stabbing clarity they had somehow manipulated her into marrying.

When she was in Carlos's presence a light went off, as though his possessing her extinguished an inner fire. A lifetime of servitude to a man like Carlos would slowly kill her. One way or another he would take her from Carlos Torres. One way or another he would free her of a bad mistake.

He owed her that much at least.

COMPULSION

All human actions have one or more of
these seven causes: chance, nature, compulsions,
habit, reason, passion, desire

~ Aristotle ~

FIGHTING BACK TEARS RUBY SUNK INTO THE soft leather seats of Carlos's sturdy, solid, conservative Chrysler 300c SRT8. *Damn Oliver for coming back into my life just when everything was under control.* Ruby tossed her head slightly to stop an errant tear from rolling down her face and betraying her.

"Where were you?" Carlos asked as he sat, his back rigid, in the driver's seat, his voice sounding a warning.

"Nowhere important," she smiled more brightly than she felt. She avoided Carlos's penetrating gaze as tears rimmed her eyes.

"You sure?" He looked at her down the wide bridge of his nose, then pulled her hand toward him and gripped it tightly.

Ruby didn't move.

"Oliver wanted to show me something. I couldn't say no." Her words, though true, sounded hollow.

His dark eyes blackened.

"Nothing happened," she lied, knowing she couldn't possibly tell him the truth. He would be enraged. He would be incensed. He would do something they'd all live to regret.

Carlos turned the key in the ignition, the engine fired at once, purring like a lion. Evidently satisfied with her answer, he tracked his finger down her quivering neck with controlled deliberateness.

Ruby straightened and fixed her gaze on the neon lights illuminating the dashboard. Her mind flashed back to her encounter with Oliver. The way his lips brushed her ears. The way his eyes pierced her soul. The way every neuron in her brain, and every cell in her heart, flashed lovers red as his mouth claimed hers.

Carlos reached over and stroked her thigh.

Ruby grimaced involuntarily, painfully aware of the contrast between Carlos's and Oliver's touch. It was like comparing nylon to silk.

She closed her eyes and tried to dislodge the guilt she felt. She should have resisted. She should never have let him steal a kiss. Passion had rendered her powerless. Passion had made her feel happy. And now she must dislodge Oliver from her mind.

As she buckled her seat belt, she wondered if she could ever manufacture the feelings for Carlos that Oliver unleashed.

Those feelings which rose unbridled, deep within her loin, heart, and head in Oliver's presence. Feelings stamped with a powerful authenticity that seared through her heart and branded her as belonging only to Oliver.

"I think we should bring the wedding forward," Carlos said, his voice a decisive command.

"Wedding?" she said, struggling to keep the alarm from her voice. Good god, they weren't even formally engaged yet and now he was fast-tracking a wedding.

Wedding. The word was a powerfully stark reminder of her impending loss of freedom. As a girl, she had dreamed of an all-consuming love and a romantic proposal under a starry sky.

Ruby bit her lip and swallowed her disappointment. Her mother's words bored into the night, 'Romantic love is for fools, fading like the beauty of youth. Sacrifice and family honor is a woman's duty. *Your duty.* You owe us that.'

Ruby reluctantly conceded her mother was right. She'd fallen head over high heels in foolish romantic love with Oliver once and it had only brought heartache. She would not make that mistake twice.

As Carlos accelerated down the drive she turned her head briefly. Oliver stood in the entranceway, his arms folded, staring at her. Ruby's stomach knotted as her eyes were captured by his smoldering jade-green gaze.

She threw Oliver a derisive glance. Some men just weren't worth all the trouble. She knew when she married she wanted it to be with a man who really wanted her, not a man who wanted what others coveted, a man who had one foot in their relationship and the other primed for escape.

Carlos laid his hand in hers, and she closed her fingers around his soft palm, sadly aware that not one single part of her body tingled or ached or fired with passion.

Oliver's prophecy tolled in her ears. 'You can't lie to yourself, not for long.'

The futility of the warning struck into her like a knife tearing silk. Smooth, quick, irreparable.

Until now she'd been doing a perfectly good job of deceiving herself. But how long could she keep up the pretense?

12

LIVER'S BROW KNITTED TO-GETHER AS HE watched Ruby drive away. He placed his hand on his chest in a vain attempt to control the quickness of his heart which beat so fast he thought it might explode. What the hell was he feeling? It was completely irrational. Dangerous. Compelling.

He wanted her, desired her, wished to possess her—and there was no way he was going to let that happen.

He shook his head at his weakness. This was not the time nor place for sexual distraction. It was a time for discipline. His sister's life depended upon it.

Oliver returned to the house, and strode to his room. He walked over to the walk-in wardrobe, reached high into it, and pulled down a worn backpack.

"My lucky charm," he said as he ran his fingers gently over the worn blue canvas. It wasn't that he was superstitious or even believed in all that hoo-ha about talismans, four-leaf clovers, rabbit's feet, or any kind of amulet. But he had to admit something was reassuring about the feel of that pack beneath his skin. It was as though each time he touched it, the luck of the gods was on his side.

He could afford the most sophisticated gear on the market, but this pack was lucky, he thought recalling the many life-threatening expeditions it had hauled him through.

His hand moved across the fabric protectively as his gaze took in every stain, every crease, every tear. For a few brief moments, he mourned the grandfather he'd barely known. A warm ripple coursed through his spine as he touched one of the few pieces that had been handed down the generations.

He began to fill its cavity with socks, underwear, net hoops, net handles, neatly folded glassine envelopes in which to store his prize catches. He piled in his binoculars, somber clothing to detract attention and blend in with the environment, quick-dry trousers with zip-off legs that converted into shorts to help temper the tropical heat whilst he tramped amongst wild, virgin, vegetation.

He rifled through his first aid kit, making sure he was aptly prepared in case, god forbid, he found himself at nature's mercy and zipped it into the front pocket. An equally disturbing thought jackknifed through his mind.

What if Ruby or her family got wind of his mission? The butterfly was on her family land in Mexico. Ruby lived in New York, he reasoned, she wouldn't even know he was there. But her meddling family—that was a different story.

Her family hated him, and any residual feelings of affection Ruby may still harbor for him would be shot by his unwelcome intrusion.

Oliver rose to his feet like some great bird of prey. It was a risk he had no choice but to take. He couldn't let the Diaz family get in the way of saving his sister.

13

HOW COULD HE HAVE FLIRTED SO outrageously with her? Ruby twisted a great wad of drawing paper into a tight knot, screwing her nose at the smell. Oliver was a swine, a flirt, and a degenerate, and she hated him.

He was a commitment-phobic, nothing but trouble. Trouble wasn't what she needed. More toxic glue covered paper was flung savagely into the rubbish bin.

But gradually the swift, vicious movements of her hands slowed. Her mind wandered to Oliver and his beautiful butterflies.

She envied the passion with which he lived his life.

Carlos's voice calling to her from downstairs, shouting above the grating roar of the televised soccer, snapped her thoughts back to reality. Carlos and she may not share many interests but he did offer her the security that she craved.

"I'm up here," she called, as Carlos came in search of her.

As he glanced around the room, his eyes lingering on the disorganized piles of drawings and architecture books on her desk, Ruby thought with a pang how disinterested he looked.

He walked to her desk and held up the preparatory drawing she'd been sketching of her plans to transform her family's land in Mexico into an eco-lodge and sanctuary for children raised in care.

"This is interesting." His monotonous tone told her he thought the curving forms and rammed earth architecture anything but interesting. Her heart sunk as he set it down dismissively.

"Do you always have to make such a mess?" he pursed his lips as he looked at her stained fingers.

Ruby listened to him tell her about his day and of all the social events lined up for them to attend. She noted he asked nothing about her day, as though deeming anything she did as insignificant.

"Come on, go get pretty. We've got a state banquet to attend. I want to show you off," he said.

She grimaced, tired of being a piece of showcase jewelry, a pretty bauble for others to admire. She wanted to contribute more to the world than a pretty smile. She wanted to work with purpose. She wanted to escape the mundane.

She slumped in her chair. She wanted the impossible. But she wouldn't let her current situation stop her planning a way to make her dreams come true.

"What is all this in aid of anyway?" he said glancing around her studio, pointing at her sketches and wooden architectural models.

How many times did she have to tell him about her dreams for him to care? Was her mother right, was it selfish to expect him to care about the same things that filled her heart with joy?

People didn't have to marry their likeness, she reminded herself. If they did people wouldn't make the comment that opposites attract. And there was no doubt that Carlos and she were opposite in all ways. But his sudden interest caught her off guard.

She hesitated for a moment before answering, uncertain of his response, "I've told you before, but you've been so busy with your career you've probably forgotten. It's my dream," she said simply. "For an eco-reserve and animal sanctuary back home in Mexico," she said, deliberately not mentioning how the animals would help her to provide comfort and care for traumatized and neglected kids.

Carlos hated children. After the specialists had

told her a virus left her unable to have her own kids, she hadn't tried to change his mind.

"I've told you," he interrupted, "I never want to go back to that hell-hole. I've worked my whole life just to get out of that wretched place." He pulled her to her feet. "You know I will always provide for you," he said, his voice softening.

Ruby looked out of the window at the asphalt and neon lights and the ant-like figures scrambling along the Manhattan streets below. She wrapped her arms around herself. She felt so disconnected from the urban landscape. She yearned to be closer to nature, to walk barefoot upon the earth—she yearned to go home.

"Once we are married your family's financial woes will be over," he reassured her, "the land will be—" he swallowed as though ingesting a secret he deemed unfit for her consumption. "—you will be secure. Your family secure. Now put all that nonsense away."

She pushed her drawings away and painted a smile on her lips. But she felt no gladness.

He stood there admiring her, "I've missed you," he said softly. It had been months since he approached her, she assumed it was because of work pressures. To be honest she'd been grateful. His distance had given her some much-needed space. But now he took her hand and led her from her treasured room, her sanctuary, the one place she could truly be herself.

The only question was why now? Like a fox, could he scent Oliver's claim on her?

He led her into their bedroom. Loosening the pins from her hair, he spread her spiraling locks in his hands. He lay her on the bed, methodically unbuttoning, unbuckling, unhooking the clothing which separated their flesh.

She pushed thoughts of Oliver from her mind while he sated himself, until at last, he fell asleep against her shoulder for a few minutes, his arm under her head, a tired, ambitious man with an accelerating political career. A man her family wished her to marry. A man she should feel something for.

But something made her want to weep.

She glanced guiltily at Carlos as she thought of Oliver and recalled the way his lips had nearly claimed hers. She felt her body stiffen and tremble as she folded into the memory.

She stared blindly down at the trace of drawing ink beneath her fingernails, hot tears clogging her eyes as she faced the unpalatable truth. Dangerous, reckless, arrogant, Oliver was everything she despised.

Yet she wanted him and had no idea how to keep pushing him from her mind. Would going home to Mexico provide the distance that she needed?

She would never know unless she went. Tomorrow she would pack her bags and leave—just for a week to clear her head, she resolved, burying herself in the sheets.

DESIRE

To burn with desire and keep quiet about it is the
greatest punishment we can bring on ourselves

~ Federico García Lorca ~

14

RUBY HESITATED AT THE GATEWAY TO HER parents' *estancia*. Her heart leaped at the familiar scent of clear country air and exotic blooms covering the land. Here was a chance to flee fate. A chance before it was too late, to pry herself free and determine her own destiny where neither family nor duty had influence.

She turned briefly and surveyed the sprawling landscape. The sea of soothing, contrasting greens momentarily distracted her from the mountainous task that lay ahead. Dreams. Reckless dreams, she reminded herself.

Her family were broke. She would never inherit the wealth she needed. She must put duty first. Once powerful the Diaz family had carried much respect in Mexico and with her intended betrothal to Carlos Torres, her family fortune would be restored and the family *estancia* saved.

Slipping off her shoes she stepped onto the pasture and burrowed her toes into the freshly cut grass, a habit she'd maintained for years to re-anchor herself to the land after so much time in New York's sprawling metropolis. She closed her eyes, raised her face to the cloudless sky, and inhaled the sweet country air.

The deafening sound of crushing gravel shattered the silence. Horse steps, calculated in their purpose drew upon her.

"Well, if the prodigal daughter hasn't returned." Her stepbrother's lips curved into a snarl.

"Antonio!" she said, her eyes wide with fright.

His eyes burned with accusation as he dismounted from his black stallion. He raised his right cheek toward her and tapped it lightly with his finger.

She stepped dutifully toward him and kissed him lightly on both cheeks.

"I didn't expect to see you until the cattle muster next week," Ruby said sweetly beneath a nervous smile.

"Next week might be too late," he said abruptly. "The wolves are circling. You of all people must understand," he added making no effort to mask the contempt in his voice.

Ruby nodded. She dug her toes firmly into the soil, "Yes, I'm well aware."

"Why then," Antonio demanded, "do you risk everything?"

Ruby stepped back and looked at him through uncertain eyes.

"You were seen with Oliver Hart," he growled, his voice while measured carried a threat.

A question formed on her lips. A question she dare not ask. *How did you know? Are you spying on me?*

"What the hell are you playing at Ruby? That man is trouble. Always was. Always will be."

"I had nothing to do with it. Carlos wanted something Oliver owned. He took me to him. It was not my idea. Carlos does what he wants," she said, fixing her eyes firmly on her brother. "Oliver means nothing," she murmured, averting her gaze and praying that he didn't register the lilt in her voice that called her a liar

Antonio closed his cracked fingers around her arm, "Make sure he knows that. Do you hear? The last thing we need is him ruining everything."

Ruby nodded solemnly.

"Don't forget—" he hissed, releasing his grip. His eyes narrowed and his lips curled like a wild dog tormenting its prey. "Don't forget what will happen if you fail," he called as he mounted his horse.

Ruby fell silent as she watched him ride away. A cloud of dust billowed behind him as he galloped toward the stables, trailing like deadly ash.

She bit her lower lip and unclenched her delicate fingers. The peace and tranquility she'd felt was quickly consumed by her step-brother's controlling, unpredictable temper.

She took a deep breath to settle her trembling belly and let out a big sigh.

This was not going to be easy, she decided as she hopped back into the rented jeep and drove toward the house, along a sweeping driveway lined with hundreds of jacaranda trees blooming like soft purple clouds. As she caught sight of crocuses clustered together in the far flowerbed like butterflies gathered to lap at a puddle, her thoughts returned to Oliver, and the heaviness she'd felt in her heart returned anew.

But as the historic hacienda came into sight her spirits soared. The 19th century stone building shone like a precious jewel in the midday sun. It nestled happily atop a hill with magnificent views of the ocean below and the surrounding lush, tropical countryside.

Now my soul can soar, she mused happily.

As the jeep continued its climb and drew closer the salmon pink plaster walls and the terracotta tiled roof came into view, warming her soul with its ageless grace. The colonial pillars supporting the veranda reminded her of an ancient Roman bathhouse upon which scarlet bougainvilleas trailed happily.

Ruby smiled like a child greeting a dearly loved, but seldom seen, grandmother. Feelings of excitement entwined with worry for the future coursed through her body. How could she ever let *Casa Rosa* go? She knew with clarity she must do everything in her power to keep it safe.

Surely she could make her family understand there were alternatives to the course they so determinedly pursued. A course that would deny her freedom, her dreams, her passions.

As she stepped down from the jeep onto the stone cobbled tiles and walked slowly toward the entrance she wondered with rising anxiety if for once her family would be receptive to her ideas.

Ruby paused briefly to pick at a piece of peeling plaster and rubbed it wistfully in her finger before discarding it gently upon the ground. As she approached the ornately carved wooden door she paused to collect her thoughts, bracing herself for what she must do.

Ruby placed her hand slowly on the wrought-iron handle and took a deep breath. Freedom, she knew, was a gift she would never know until she fought for it.

The heavy three-meter mahogany double doors suddenly sprung open. Maria, the servant who had raised her since birth, bustled out, her chubby arms held wide open. A smile spread across her face. She wore a pale gray dress with a lace apron.

"Ruby" she cried, smothering her face with wet kisses.

Ruby smiled and allowed herself to be swallowed by Maria's generous bosom, welcoming her familiarity.

Maria took a few steps back upon the terracotta tiles, "Let me take a look at you." Her eyes swept quickly from Ruby's face to her feet and then back to her face as she read her emotions. She stepped forward again, reached out, lifted Ruby's chin with her plump forefinger and looked deeply into her eyes.

"Why so sad?"

Ruby's mouth curved tightly, "I'm tired, that's all. Everything's fine." She averted her eyes from Maria's probing gaze.

"Is that wonderful Carlos keeping you up too late?" Maria said, winking. "Think how your life will be. Ahhh, and your papa so proud. So happy his daughter can find happiness."

Ruby smiled and looked sad, both at once.

"Yes, Father will be happy. Happy now I can finally be useful to him," she said quietly, the soft timbre of her voice masking her growing apprehension.

"Your father loves you, Ruby. All he has ever wanted is to secure your future."

"By deciding my fate? By making me feel guilty for wanting a life of my own?"

"Have courage, my love."

"I'm trying, but so much is at stake."

Maria wrapped her arms around her and hugged her tightly.

"You must always listen to your heart," Maria said softly.

Ruby gazed solemnly at the tiled floor. She'd never thought with her heart. She'd learned to contain her feelings from an early age. Listening to her heart had only brought trouble, just as it was doing now as it cried out for Oliver.

"It is not easy to follow your own path. Easy is to do what others want," Maria continued as though sensing the battle between emotion and logic, duty and desire, that waged war within Ruby's overactive brain, "but the heart is your faithful servant . . . if you allow it."

A wave of sadness washed over Maria's face momentarily, then lifted like a cloud passing over the sun. Ruby looked with surprise at Maria's moistened eyes. Ruby scolded herself silently for being ungrateful for the threads of freedom she did have, freedom a servant on low wages would never know.

"Maria, I'm sorry. I sound ungrateful. But I'm grateful—" she began tentatively. She wanted to say how thankful she was to have been adopted by the Diaz's, to have been given a home, a beautiful home, but she couldn't shake the hurt that she'd never felt wanted.

Maria lifted her chin, kissed her on the forehead and took Ruby determinedly by the hand. "Come, your mother will be excited to see you."

Ruby bit her lip. *Somehow she doubted it.*

15

S HE STEPPED BAREFOOT ONTO THE RUST-
colored Mayan tiles, drawing strength from the smooth, natural stone beneath her feet. As Maria led her quickly down the wide hallway, she glided along the terracotta tiles. Eighteen foot high ceilings, with exposed beams and rafters, stonewalls, and hand-carved tropical hardwood furniture, flawlessly drew attention to their Mexican culture and evoked the splendor of past eras.

There was something solidly reassuring about the treasured possessions that had been handed down through the generations, Ruby reflected as she ran her hand across the smooth, polished surface of an antique table lining the hall.

She felt as though each heirloom contained

the spirit of their creators, reaching out to her in solidarity, and offering her more comfort than she'd ever found in the arms of those that lived.

"Señora, your daughter is here," Maria announced formally from the periphery of the kitchen. Ruby wasn't surprised to find her mother there. Her mother loved to cook.

Joy Diaz looked up briefly. Her lips stretched into a stiff smile before returning her gaze to the floured marble benchtop.

"You look like you've put on weight."

Ruby drew a deep breath. Her mother was in one of those moods.

"A little," Ruby said, not wanting to risk more criticism.

"Sit down, stop hovering. You know how I feel about people in the kitchen." She gestured with flour-covered hands toward the 10-seater, wooden table in the center of the kitchen, then turned and reached into the wood-fired oven.

Ruby held her hands over her rumbling stomach as her mother withdrew a hot tray of freshly cooked tortillas. She looked derisively over Ruby's shoulder toward the kitchen door, and back to Ruby again, her brow creasing.

"Where is Carlos?" she asked coolly.

"He couldn't come. He has business."

"Business? That boy always is always working. We never see him."

"We have something else in common," Ruby said softly, picking at the edges of her tortilla.

"You need to watch yourself, Ruby. Men like Carlos need looking after," she said sternly, looking down her aristocratic nose. "What could be more important than the business he has with this family? Everything is okay I hope?"

Ruby's shoulders knotted with tension, "Yes, everything is okay," she said more brightly than she felt. "It's Carlos—he is so busy with his campaign, I hardly see him."

"It is better not to expect too much," her mother said sharply, noticing the disappointment in her daughter's voice.

"I know, it's just that . . ."

"Just what?" Her mother's voice sounded a warning.

Ruby's eyes darted beyond her mother's reproachful gaze. As she watched the white swans glide gracefully upon the lake, she felt strangely envious of their freedom and their love. Mates for life, how was it possible?

"Just what, Ruby?" her mother demanded.

Ruby took a deep breath, summoning courage as she did so. "Mama," she began tentatively. Okay, here it goes. "What should true love feel like?"

"True love? True love is a freshly baked plate of tortillas," she said, pushing them beyond Ruby's reach.

Ruby folded her arms and shifted on her seat. Her attempt to draw closer to her mother and her plea for guidance once again escaped her.

"It's just, I'm not sure of my feelings for Carlos," she persisted. Taking another deep breath, her voice trembled slightly as she spoke again, "I'm not sure that marrying him is the only answer."

Impatience rose in her mother's voice like steam escaping from a pressure cooker, "You watch too many movies. Always filling your head with romantic visions of happily ever after. Always the dreamer. Life is not a fairytale, my girl. *Life is not a Mills and Boon.* Life is family. Dedication. Honor. Sacrifice."

She rose from the table and walked briskly to the kitchen window. "Our families have business," she said sharply, fixing her gaze on the row of terracotta urns filled with prickly cacti.

"I know," Ruby said gently, rising to her feet and walking toward her mother. Her vocal cords trembled, quivering as she tried to summon the courage to share her feelings. "I think I can find a way for all of us to be happy. A way that needn't involve me marrying for money, a way ..."

Joy Diaz stretched the pastry over the cold

marble bench, her lips pursed as she clenched the ends of the rolling pin, raised it abruptly, and slammed it down with a chilling thud. She spun around, facing Ruby with a hostility that threw her.

"We need this marriage! Don't be so selfish!"

Ruby looked briefly into her mother's face and tried to understand her attack. She had not even let her finish. She had not even heard her ideas. A pro when it came to manipulation her mother had instead labeled her as selfish and made Ruby feel instantly guilty.

Ruby's eyes stung. She fought back tears and resolved to put her mother's heightened brittleness down to stress. The strain of trying to support her ailing father. The worry of trying to keep the creditors from the door. The pressure of trying to run the ranch on a shoestring. It hurt less.

Why else would she be so cruel?

Joy Diaz pursed her lips. "Considering all that we have done for you, all we have given you, is it too much to ask you to do something for us? Is it too much for you to do as women throughout history have done and continue to do—to marry because it is convenient? Or are you better than everyone else?"

Ruby shook her head. "No."

"We agree on something then. Forget romantic notions of love. Save these for a night at the movies or a good book. Carlos is a clever man. An ambitious man. A rich man. You will not find better."

"Yes, he is, and he deserves to be happy. We both do." Ruby faced her mother with uncharacteristic defiance. "But I don't love him as I should."

Her mother's eyes darkened. "Love? What's love got to do with it?" Her eyes narrowed. "Has something changed?" she hissed through pursed lips.

Ruby knew no good would come of mentioning Oliver. No good would come from sharing the unexpected passions that rippled through her body when he touched her. No good would come from replaying memories of a love once shared but then so ruthlessly abandoned.

"Nothing has changed," Ruby said flatly.

Carlos was still dependable, still reliable. Still determined to have her as his wife. And although it pained her to concede the truth, she knew her mother was right. They needed this marriage. They needed a promise-keeper—not someone who would abandon them.

"Good," Joy Diaz said, rubbing flour from her hands. "Next time don't come home without Carlos," she said firmly. "I assume it hasn't escaped you?"

Ruby's brows knitted in a perplexed frown.

"Men are not in plentiful supply. You must never let a man like him out of your sight or someone will steal him. Besides," she continued her voice softening as she sensed Ruby's resignation, "it will do your father good to see you both together as our families have always intended."

Two butterflies dancing joyfully past the window caught Ruby's eye. Part of her sensed it was futile to attempt to change the course of fate, yet something deep within her wished it didn't have to feel such a burden.

Now was not the time to speak about love. But perhaps talk of money, a topic always on their minds, would bridge the widening gulf between them. There was no reason that just because she was marrying she need forsake her dream.

"About my idea." Ruby's voice grew louder and her conviction deeper as the passion carrying her words grew like sugar cane in the sun. "I have an idea for the *estancia*, to make it financially viable."

"Bahh!" Her stepbrother scoffed, striding into the kitchen and wrapping his stocky arms around his mother, kissing the back of her neck tenderly before turning to Ruby. "Bahhh, to your ideas. Ideas don't put food on the table. Ideas don't pay the mortgage." He pulled over a chair from the dining table, slammed it down and sat, shoveling tortilla into his mouth.

"I can make this idea work," Ruby said quietly,

confidence ebbing as her brother's mocking suffocated her passion.

"Business? Business is a man's domain. Stick to your knitting. Stick to your hobbies."

Silent fury quietly simmering within Ruby suddenly rose like a flooded stream, "Women all over the world run businesses, and have done for years you ignorant moron—and what's more their men proudly encourage them. What have you ever done to bring money into this home?" she challenged.

"Don't talk to your brother like that!" her mother scolded, going to her son's side. "He tries. The recession is not his fault. And he is right. We need money, not ideas. I can't pay the creditors with ideas. Just like I can't pay them with tortillas."

Ruby swallowed a terrible desire to tell them to go to hell. But she knew she couldn't. They were her family. And even if most times she felt like an outsider, like she was a mistake, the cold truth was they had adopted her. They were the only family to have wanted her after endless foster homes. And *Casa Rosa* was the only place where she had ever felt she belonged.

While she couldn't understand why most of the time she seemed to be an annoyance, she didn't want to fight them and be disowned.

The thought of having no one to call her family exerted a strong constraining force on her. She was afraid. Not just of losing her family but losing her beloved *Casa Rosa*.

Her family was highly dysfunctional, she thought ruefully. But she knew other families were too—Oliver Hart's included. The knowledge gave her a small degree of consolation. And while Ruby wished she'd been encouraged to expect more for herself, instead of being criticized, her quick, incisive mind, suffocated by years of criticism, her caring nature exploited and turned against her, her soul suppressed as though she was a virus, Oliver's success was testament to the truth that hardship can make you stronger.

She wanted to scream, 'It's my life. I'll do what I want, marry who I want, love who I want.' Instead, she stood dutifully, deferring to her family's wishes, just as she had eight years earlier when they'd made her give up Oliver. But that didn't mean she couldn't dream and scheme. She would gain her freedom, and she would repay the debt she owed them. What she didn't know was how.

16

SOON HER LIFE WOULD NOT BE HER OWN.

Ruby urged her stallion on as the distant thunder rolled closer. A deep violet blush, the color of bruised over-ripe merlot grapes stained the sky.

"Go, boy. Go," Ruby cried as they raced across the lush expanse. Galloping across her beloved land on a pure white horse was the most thrilling feeling in the world.

More like flying, Ruby thought, as she urged Pegasus faster. Soon the sun would be setting, the light too dim to go further, but for now they were able to enjoy the freedom together.

The thrill of this powerful animal pounding the Mexican soil made her feel invincible. If she was not so connected to the land she would ride like the wind far from her fate and free herself from the sacrifice that lay ahead.

As she approached the brow of the hill she pulled on the reigns and gently brought Pegasus to a stop. She gazed wistfully down upon the verdant valley. A wave of nostalgia swept over her as she recalled riding with her grandfather to this same spot so many times, so many years ago. 'One day this land will be yours,' he'd said.

Ruby brow wrinkled. It seemed as far-fetched then as it did now. A woman in her patriarchal family would never inherit a grain of rice let alone a huge thousand-acre sprawling ranch. Less so now they were broke.

She wished she did not have to marry the son of a wealthy landowner to appease her family and save their land. She wished instead that she could marry for love. But time was against her. She clenched her teeth. She must find another way. But how?

Storm clouds merged with the gathering dusk, enveloping Ruby in an ominous light. She glanced at her watch which dangled on a loose gold chain from her wrist. 7:18pm. She should head home before rain approached and the dark curtain of night fell.

The sound of flapping wings thundered through the humid air as a flock of birds swooped past racing for home as if panicked.

The stallion shied, leaping sideways, and threw back his head, his nostrils twitching violently.

"There, there, Pegasus," she said softly, pulling on the reins to steady him. "It's only birds, no need to worry."

Worries of her own clung to her mind like irritated wasps she couldn't shake. She had resigned herself to her relationship with Carlos until Oliver had turned up nipping at her conscience with irritating persistence.

Aching need washed over her. Biting down on her bottom lip she forced herself to swallow the unpalatable combination of regret and desire.

Her family was relying on her. The future of her beloved *Casa Rosa* at stake.

A loud rumble quaked through the air. Ruby glanced around her as a flash of lightning zigzagged its fiery light across the valley, illuminating everything in its path.

"What the—" she gripped the horse's belly with trembling knees, and clenched the toughened leather reins as a rapid movement in the tropical bush below jolted her senses. "Who's there?"

Ruby heard only silence at first and then a loud crack that sent shockwaves through the evergreens. Her heart quaked through her chest.

There was no mistaking the tall, muscular, athletic figure swiftly moving deftly through the scrub.

No mistaking the chiseled jaw and supremely toned physique. No mistaking the mop of dark, unruly hair that bounced jauntily through the growth.

Oliver!

What the hell was he doing here? How dare he trespass on their land? Recovering from her shock and shaken by white-hot fury. Ruby gritted her teeth and spurred her horse down the hill.

Clearly startled by the noise, Oliver looked up. For a brief moment his eyes met hers. An unwelcome tingle surged through her body, mingling with the torrent of raging adrenaline.

Ruby's eyes narrowed as she saw him throw the object he'd been brandishing into the scrub. His mouth pressed into a firm line and everything about his face was suddenly brutally hard—his aggressive jaw, the glint in his eyes and the square set of his shoulders.

Another bolt of lightning sliced through the warm, balmy air. It struck a tree ahead of her, causing a limb to crash to the ground. Startled, Pegasus whinnied, then reared up in fright.

Ruby instinctively gripped tighter and clung to his powerful neck. Terrified the horse bolted down the steep hill. As she struggled to maintain her precarious grip Oliver rushed up the hill toward her.

"I'll catch you!" he said, running beside her, as she neared low-lying scrub.

"Jump!"

There was no other option. Without hesitating she fell into his arms. His powerful arms shouldered the full impact of her weight before he fell back into the long, meadow grass, holding her to him, cushioning her fall with his body.

17

DAMN! WHAT THE HELL WAS SHE DOING IN Mexico? Oliver gritted his teeth, steeling himself against the melody of desire and irritation coursing through his veins. Just his luck, running into Ruby on the first day of his quest.

If only he hadn't been so heroic. If only protecting others wasn't so ingrained in his psyche. If only someone else had been there in that moment to play rescuer. If only she'd stayed on her damned horse.

If only she wasn't so irresistible.

A rare smile escaped as he gazed at her, her wild curls splayed around her head like serpents, her soft sensuous lips pressed into a furious, totally sexy pout.

It was irritating how readily women fell into his arms. But Ruby was different—clearly falling for him wasn't something she relished nor enjoyed. Her fierce independence and resilience set her apart from all the other prima donnas and self-absorbed women who had plummeted upon his doorstep over the years.

A frisson of unbridled desire galloped through his loins. He liked strong, independent women and he loved a challenge. Combining the two excited him—for a night or two at least.

What was he thinking? Ruby Diaz had always been a keeper. Hadn't he sworn to avoid emotional entanglement? Why then was the intoxicating urge to claim her as his own so hard to fight?

A siren-like warning blasted through his mind, *keep your distance. Keep your head.*

"Are you okay?" he said, noticing with alarm the shaky timbre of his voice as she rolled off him.

"No, I'm not okay. What in hell are you doing here, Oliver?"

～

"Right now I'm making sure you're not hurt."

"That wasn't what I asked," Ruby said, summoning enough fury to mask the flush of excitement that threatened to betray her as she propped herself on her elbows.

"Let me help you."

"I don't need your help. I'm fine,"Ruby muttered beneath clenched teeth, steeling herself against the jolt of pain that shot through her foot.

"I need to make sure my horse is alright," Ruby searched the hillside, glad of something other than Oliver to focus on.

She tried to stand then fell back against the long, soft grass as splintering pain shot through her ankle. Her pride and her body ached in unison. She closed her eyes and wished a black hole would open below and swallow her quickly.

"I see you haven't lost your willful stubbornness." A broad smirk illuminated his face, flooding Ruby's body with a warmth that unnerved her.

"Lay back and stay back," he said, his low voice rich with tenderness. The unfamiliarity of it surprised and unsettled her. No one had ever shown her such kindness.

Surely he'd turn off the charm any minute now. He'd tell her to get a grip, pick herself up and stop feeling sorry for herself, just like everyone else close to her did.

Except he was spending too much time playing doctor to even give her a chance to feel sorry. Which she wouldn't anyway. She'd learned from an early age that vulnerability led to rejection.

A shiver coursed through her veins as his powerful, masculine hands pulled off her boots and with a lightness of touch that surprised her as he pressed upon the bone of her slim ankle.

His hands felt warm, soft—dare she admit it, sensual? His fingers traveled the length of her toned denim encased legs, toward the top of her thigh.

She averted her eyes, not wishing to encourage him, but her trembling body betrayed her with hot, liquid desire as his fingers continued their march.

"Not an inch more!" The words sent a damp counter-charge through the air as she recovered from the shock of the fall.

"You can't seriously think I'd take advantage of you," he said, laying on the disbelief far too heavily. Something dangerous flickered in his eyes as he held up his hands in surrender. "This isn't seduction, it's first aid."

Oliver scanned the rapidly darkening sky. "I'm certain it's just a sprain but we need to get you home." He looked up briefly as dusky violet clouds drizzled a shower of sultry tropical late evening mist upon them.

"I'll find my own way home," she said, pushing free of his firm clasp. Whatever happened her family must never know he was there.

"It's a long walk back. Especially if you're hobbling," he said, pointing to her horse disappearing in the distance.

The stupid idiot didn't even try to catch Pegasus, Ruby cursed under her breath.

As night began to fall he looked rugged and dangerous, his soft mouth now firm with determination. Oliver's eyes blazed with a flash of rebelliousness. How could she convince him she didn't need him to play heroics? How could she convince him to leave her alone? More importantly, how could she get rid of him?

Reluctantly she took his outstretched hand and allowed him to pull her gently to her feet. She winched as her ankle gave out from under her. As she stumbled Oliver reached a strong, protective arm around her waist. He drew her close to him, allowing her to use his powerful body as her crutch.

Ruby shivered involuntarily as he lifted her into his arms.

He shifted his weight and threw her over his shoulders. She'd never felt so vulnerable and so ridiculous. Her eyes drifted to his broad shoulders and muscular back, her eyes lingering on his Levi jeans and the hardened outline of his firm buttocks.

"Promise me there will be no trouble," she called over his shoulder awkwardly.

If Ruby hadn't been hanging over his back she

was sure she would've have noticed a wry smile settle on his lips.

"Who me—trouble?" he replied unconvincingly as he walked determinedly toward the ranch.

TEMPTATION

Forgive us our sins, for we also forgive everyone
who sins against us. And lead us not into temptation

~ Luke 11:4 ~

18

T EMPTATION. IT'S PURE TEMPTA-
TION, RUBY reminded herself, fighting the
realization that in Oliver's arms she belonged. She knew she should resist his smoldering
glances, the raw desire she saw in his eyes to possess
her. But a persistent voice urged her to break free
from everyone's demands and honor her own needs
for once.

She had forgiven Carlos for his transgression
with his campaign manager last June, and she had
accepted his explanation that it was a meaningless
fling that would never happen again. Wives and
husbands were always forgiving each other, it
seemed.

Besides, didn't she owe it to herself to prove beyond all doubt that what she felt for Oliver was a

mistaken belief, a lingering legacy of their unresolved past, before she committed herself to Carlos for the rest of her life?

Absolutely, she resolved. She would claim this chance encounter and make it a night to remember —and forget.

"The *casita* is closer," she'd told him as she guided him to the guest house on the edge of the estate. It was her private escape. The one place where she could truly be herself. The only place they wouldn't be discovered.

He didn't protest. In fact, she sensed by the way his body pulsed he was positively pleased. Secretly she was pleased too. She could do as she pleased and be answerable to no one.

They would have just this one night. That was all, she vowed as he carried her past the floating clusters of trumpet-shaped flowers and plump clumps of hibiscus surrounding the guesthouse. With their melody of exquisite blue-lavender and riotous pink colors, they were at once both peaceful and intense.

Breathe. Breathe, she told herself as Oliver opened the door and lay her gently upon the bed. Eight years had passed and, while she was no longer a virgin, she knew instinctively that sex with Oliver would be explosive.

Mother have mercy, she muttered under her

breath, biting her lip as he pulled his fitted tee-shirt, damp from the shower of rain, over his head, and then strode out of his jeans.

As he stood before her, his toned, taunt, rock-hard muscles glistening under the moonlight, her heart halted. He was sleek-skinned, powerfully made—and huge. *Everywhere.*

Her lips curved into a tight, anxious smile. She couldn't control the tension that stiffened her muscles and dried her throat. Her body pulsated with anticipation as he moved toward her, his eyes narrowed in primal desire.

Succumbing to temptation and deciding to sleep with Oliver had been a foolish, uncharacteristically impulsive idea. She was way out of her comfort zone. Out of balance. Out of control.

Snap out of it, Ruby reminded herself. You have to do this. It's just about tonight. No longer. No shorter. You have to rid him from your psyche. Permanently.

She inhaled a long deep low breath through her parted lips and nestled into the soft cotton sheets as her confusion lifted, buoyed by the knowledge that like a short summer fling, there would be no next time.

Having sex would exorcise Oliver permanently from her mind. At least that's what she kept trying to convince herself.

Oliver stood firm. Watching, not moving—except for his chest, which rose and fell rapidly. She heard him panting, more breathlessly than when he had carried her here. She smelt the musky odor of his manliness.

He leaned over her, his gaze unflinching, until only an inch or so separated them. As she searched his expression his gaze dropped as if he didn't want her to read his mind.

He came closer still. She could feel the warmth of his breath on her cheek, his heated body only centimeters away.

She was completely at his command.

Ruby closed her eyes and prayed for mercy as he mounted her. With deft skill and lightness of touch, he swept his powerful hand beneath her back and unclasped her bra.

Her body quivered as he cupped his strong hands softly around her aching breasts. The consummate seducer, she decided as he peeled her clothes from her writhing body.

Oliver kissed her thighs with his sensual mouth His moist probing tongue slithered along her body. His right leg coiled around her left as he pulled her to him. Need, urgent and unbridled, rose inside her as he began to take control.

She lifted a heavy arm and buried her fingers in his hair, warm from his body, his skin bronzed against the paleness of her own. The pressure of her fingers raking his scalp reiterated her need and her desire and her surrender.

If she came to her senses and called a halt to it now she would never forgive herself, she concluded, as she allowed herself to be consumed by his sexual prowess. She needed someone who didn't put himself above her. She needed someone to love her like a man.

Ruby had never known such rapture. It swamped everything else, rioting through her in scintillating waves, setting her alight and anchoring her intensely in Oliver's arms, willing prisoner of his mouth and hands and the mastery of his lean, aroused body.

Outside her window, the warm, tropical breeze laden with rain danced amongst the Tibetan prayer chimes hanging from the flowering Jacaranda tree. The soft, spiritual melody fluttered through the air.

When they were both spent she lay in his arms and drowned in her guilty pleasure.

"That was amazing," he sighed, sweeping his hand beneath her neck, and pulling her gently to him.

Ruby said nothing. But felt everything. The relief of oneness she felt when her body writhed and arched in unison with him, the joy of sex that was beyond good, the fact he cared more about pleasing her than pleasuring himself. The secret pleasure she felt knowing she had taken not a small measure of control.

In return, she gave him everything, more than she had to anyone.

19

THE NIGHT FADING INTO DAWN JOLTED HER senses. Last night, they had last night, and there was to be no more. Rationally it made sense, but as she gazed upon his naked, sleeping body her heart ached and yearned for more.

He lay on his back, draped in swaths of cream muslin that hung from the canopied bed. His sculptured torso twisted slightly, revealing the tattoo coiled over his shoulder. The spirals accentuated the roundness of the muscles, enhancing his beautiful body. She trailed a finger over the intricate design which wove across the arm possessively flung over her chest, blissfully unaware of the turmoil churning within her.

Her gaze lingered over the sheets draped sensually over his naked body, enveloping his firm buttocks and muscular thighs, immortalizing his nakedness. It was as though he was a reincarnation of Michelangelo's statue of David, powerfully symbolizing strength and human beauty. Ruby dared not move, dared not breathe for fear of waking him.

The dappled sunlight streaming through the Jacaranda leaves accented the firm contours of his muscles and cast a heavenly glow.

Act cool, she said to herself as he started to stir. That's all you have to do—act cool. She had no need to feel guilty. They hadn't promised each other anything. It was a stolen moment. A moment she'd selfishly longed for since the first time they had met.

And now it was over.

Oliver doesn't care for me, she reminded herself. If she succumbed to his charm the family farm would be sold and lost to her forever. If she resisted him and kept her distance she would marry Carlos as planned. Her family would be happy and in time, if she learned to love Carlos like she should, perhaps she could be happy too.

She wondered what foolishness had driven her to put herself in such an uncompromising position. She wondered how fleeting desire had caused her to stray so far.

I don't care for you, she repeated gazing at his

sleeping body. If that was true, she thought, as her heart plummeted, why did it hurt so bad?

But she knew two things with absolute clarity.

Oliver couldn't be found. And she must honor her commitments.

FIXATION

A fixation is very stubborn: it burrows into the
brain and breaks the heart. There are many
fixations, but love is the worst

~ Isabel Allende ~

20

DAMN HER! HOW DARE RUBY DENY HIM. WITH razor-like precision Oliver brandished the machete with the force of a man possessed. He watched with satisfaction as the fallen branch splintered into tiny fragments.

Damn her and her stubborn sense of duty to hell. With the flourish of an executioner, he swung the razor-sharp blade through the thick, tangled mass of vines that covered the forest floor.

He had wasted too much time already. Oliver glanced at the sun. Full and ripe and searing hot. Perfect conditions. There was no time to waste. He must catch the butterfly today if he was to succeed in his quest.

He glanced at the compass on his watch. This should be the spot. He rested the three-meter long handle of the net against a tropical hardwood tree. Its slender trunk towered into the air like a giant fireman's pole. The arching leaves of the tree provided welcome relief from the scorching midday sun.

Only madmen and butterflies come out in this heat, Oliver chuckled, as he took off his wide-rimmed khaki hat and wiped the sweat from his brow.

He must be mad. Mad to be alone in the jungle chasing after a tiny creature. Mad to be giving his heart to a tiny object he may love forever but that would never, ever love him back.

He leaned against the tree and twisted his foot in the soil. Was it madness or fear that drove him from the arms of the most beautiful girl in the world.

Safety. Sanity. Security. At least his obsession was something tangible. Something real. Something he could control.

Unlike love.

And unlike other collecting trips this time he had a compelling purpose. Jacqui's life depended on his success.

Then he saw it. The treasure for which he was prepared to risk everything. The treasure that others coveted but none had been able to collect. The treasure that could save his sister's life.

Passion burned within him like a raging flame. He wanted to scream; to lie down on the ground and beat his fists and feet against the happy earth; to have Hope, the Papilio Esperanza, over him like a shroud while he stood, not breathing, was a dream.

Instead, he crossed his arms over his chest and stared as the butterfly flitted high amongst the canopy a giant 50 meters above.

Whatever he did he must not squander the opportunity with one emotionally out of control sweep of his net.

Other predators like wasps would not be so merciful. They would torture the beauty with their vicious barbs and poisonous sting, causing it to plummet to the ground.

Oliver would treat her with the reverence Hope deserved. After considerable effort to reach it, he would sweep the butterfly delicately in his net, carry it tenderly back down to the ground, and pray that she would lay eggs, before putting her to sleep and adding her to his collection.

She would feel no pain. He would make sure of that. He would save her from a much crueler death —unscrupulous predators who would suck her life force. And though she may never know it, her death would save his sister's life.

He gazed up the towering canopy where the butterfly flew. He sat on the ground, suddenly overcome. He had forgotten to breathe and his head hammered. The hairs on his neck stood to attention and he felt an uncontrollable, inexplicable sense of danger.

Screeching insects wouldn't shut up, nearly driving him mad with their shrill banter. On and on they relentlessly bleated. Imagining climbing to the top branches of the tree filled him with panic.

Of course he was mad. Mad and obsessed. What other person would climb so high with such a fear of heights? He gritted his teeth.

"You have to do it."

His passion and conviction urged him on. His obsessive pursuit of butterflies had taken him to the furthest corners of the world and he'd not fallen from a tree yet. He glanced up at the canopy again.

Still, it was a pretty lean, mean looking tree.

"There's nothing else for it," Oliver said obstinately, as the tell-tale spinning sensation took hold. Nothing great in the world has been achieved without passion, he encouraged himself, nothing great has been achieved without risk. He ignored the question that begged to be asked, 'So why won't you commit to Ruby?'

He jerked his head back and gulped back water, pouring the cool, refreshing, liquid down his face. He shook his head vigorously and steeled himself for the climb.

Oliver gripped the machete handle in his teeth like a pirate and draped the diameter of the net over his head. His hands free, he hooked a rope around the back circumference of the trunk, and then twisted it around his well-worn tramping boots, creating a chain that would help him shimmy his way up the trunk.

Could any place be hotter or more punishing, he thought, as he wrapped his arms tightly around the roughly textured trunk?

What was Ruby was doing now, he suddenly wondered as he recalled how her soft, supple, skin responded to his touch. He grimaced. Last night was a stark contrast to the hard, gnarly, rigid lump of living wood to which he now so foolishly clung.

His arms should have been wrapped around Ruby. His arms should have been hugging her tightly. His arms should have been drawing her to him, possessing her in a frenzied yet heartfelt embrace.

Except he wasn't, he was here. Alone.

Alone in this godforsaken, unbearably hot, hellhole. Alone, at the mercy of his skills and the unforgiving bush. Alone, fending for himself. Alone, with no one to help him should anything go wrong.

Nothing would go wrong, Oliver reminded himself. He had made sure of that. As always he'd been meticulous in his planning. As meticulous as he could be when dealing with the elements.

He gripped the tree and began to pull himself slowly upwards with sheer, stubborn brute force. He glanced up at his bulging biceps and was glad he'd placed a few more weights on at the gym to give him more muscle power.

It would be a long, slow climb. But soon the butterfly would be his. His for the taking. His for the keeping. His for Jacqui's cure.

Hugging the tree in a bear-like grip, he drew his feet up and inched his way up its length. His progress was excruciatingly slow. It had to be to avoid chafing his arms as he edged over the rough bark. He paused briefly upon branches that could hold his weight to regain his strength and with grim determination avoided looking down.

Only 10 meters to go he guessed and then he would be at the top where he would lie and wait and when the moment came he would, with any luck, take a direct swing, and net the butterfly in one skillful swoop.

That, was of course, assuming everything was going according to agenda. His plan to capture Ruby with one charmingly, skillful bedtime romp hadn't work either he mused ruefully.

In fact, since Ruby had come on the scene all his plans were fast disappearing. But giving up wasn't his style. He drew out his machete and hacked a branch away from the center of the trunk and continued forging a direct line to the canopy.

Oliver vowed not to allow himself to get distracted. First, he would get his butterfly. Then he would get the girl, taking from Carlos the woman he had no right to possess.

His ego was getting him into a spot of bother he had to concede, as a strong gust of wind whisked his hat off. Without thinking, Oliver looked down. A wave of nausea engulfed him as he watched the cap sail 20 meters to the floor, bouncing off jagged branches as it made its unplanned descent. Oliver froze and gripped the tree more tightly.

Don't look up. Don't look down, he cautioned.

21

"YOU COULD HAVE DIED."

Ruby's disapproving tone conflicted with the concern pooling in her eyes. Could it be that she cared more for him than Oliver dared let himself imagine?

"Lucky, I've got such a thick head," he shot back, grimacing as she wrapped a bandage around his head. Playing patient wasn't his idea of doctors and nurses, he mused irritably.

Oliver threw back the sheets and eased his legs out of the bed, gritting his teeth as spiking pain like great rocks of hail peppered his bruised spine. Where was his pack? It was imperative he got to it before Ruby discovered his deception. A corrugated scowl rippled across his brow.

Ruby shot him a warning look as her soft palm pushed firmly against his chest.

"You're going nowhere." She bent down and lifted his legs with a strength that surprised and aroused him. Desire coursed through his veins as her warm, tender skin connected with his.

Instant fire.

Oliver fell back reluctantly as unwanted emotion, more painful than the dull throbbing in his head, beat a discordant tune.

"You're lucky I found you."

How could he have made such a fatal error?

One minute he had the butterfly in his reach. He recalled catching it and taking it from the net. Its frail wings were damaged. The wind had most probably battered it, rendering it imperfect for his purposes but still able to fly. Oliver demanded perfection. So he'd set it free.

His next attempt had been more successful. He'd clambered down the tree, placed the Hope butterfly carefully in a large jar, ensuring she had her food plant so she could lay eggs, and placed the jar in his pack. Then he climbed that wretched tree to catch another. He had to. He couldn't leave it to chance. What if one butterfly didn't lay eggs?

He remembered seeing another one. His reach had exceeded his grasp, sending him plummeting to the jungle floor bed. The luck of the gods must have cushioned his fall plunging him into the soft, springy bushes below.

What had she seen? Oliver's eyes flew around the familiar room of the *casita* then drifted beyond the window. The sky was low and troubled. A feverish shiver coiled through his body.

"My backpack?" he asked, keeping his voice even to mask his rising anxiety. His eyes darted for the floor glancing over his bag as though it were of less relevance.

"Don't worry. I picked up everything. Nothing was left behind," she said softly in soothing, melodic tones.

Only my pride, thought Oliver as he tried to prop himself up.

He didn't want her pity, he reflected glumly. He clenched and unclenched his fists repeatedly, averting his gaze from those big blue, endless, all-seeing eyes. Eyes that seemed to see right through his rugged exterior and conflicted conscience. Eyes that seemed to see right through his veneer. Eyes that seemed to pierce through to his soul.

"Bloody weakling," he cursed as he struggled in vain.

Ruby gestured to the chair by the window. His trusty blue rucksack, worn and frayed, perched uncomfortably on the unblemished fabric, as though at any moment it could topple—like Oliver's resolve.

Oliver's gaze ricocheted between Ruby and the pack. Either she was putting up a great façade or she didn't suspect a thing. He heaved a frustrated sigh and fell back against the luxurious pillows.

Ruby's gaze intensified, flitting first to his rucksack and then back to Oliver as though trying to reach into the deep fathoms of his mind. She dipped into the antique porcelain bowl at the side of the table and withdrew a soft, cotton cloth. With long supple fingers, she wrung out the excess water.

"What a fine pair we are," she said, "Both walking wounded." The irony didn't escape him. He was as damaged as she was, they were both dragging around their childhood wounds.

Leaning dangerously close to him, she drew the cloth slowly across his brow. The smell of her skin, the sensuality of her touch, the desire he fought valiantly to suppress and the secret he knew he must keep wound his heart into a knotted mess.

Oliver's mouth went dry. How much did she know?

"I suppose you found my Playboys?" he tested, nodding in the bag's direction.

She rolled her eyes, barely masking her disdain. "Don't worry Oliver, I'm not in the least bit interested in what's in that crumby old bag."

Then, as though sensing his unusual preoccupation with the pack, her pupils dilated with hawk-like intensity. "Should I be?"

"Be my guest," he challenged, foiling his apprehension with a raspy, seductive drawl. He was sure if he came on sexy her curiosity would quickly cool. Ever since that night of passion she'd kept her distance from him.

She wrinkled her nose, her eyes hardened with the cool, detachment he'd come to expect.

"Yuck! I wouldn't touch that sack with a 20-foot magic wand. It's disgusting. When's the last time you gave it a good spring clean?"

If only she would put as much energy into loving him as she did resisting, he thought irritably.

"It's sentimental," Oliver bit back.

Ruby's eyes widened, "I didn't take you for the sentimental type."

Oliver averted his gaze. If only she knew. "So how long are you planning on keeping me in your bed," he said, steering his voice into a seductive, premeditated crawl.

Ruby's lips pressed into a firm barrier as he knew they would. She was so predictable, so desirable, he conceded, so damned addictive.

"You should be right in a few days. Then you can go. Believe me, I'm counting the nights."

He quirked an eyebrow. "I guess we're stuck with

each other until then." Oliver shot back. If only he could put aside his passion. If only he could curb his obsession.

22

HE TRIED TO STUDY HER WITH CLINICAL detachment as she tucked him into bed. It was a strangely intimate moment. For a brief shining moment, he saw what it might be like to call her his wife, Mrs. Ruby Hart. His heart surged, warmth flooding him like a day at the beach. It sounded good. Felt good. Damn. He was in trouble.

She smiled self-consciously suddenly aware of his lingering gaze. "Don't get too attached," she said softly, picking up a jug of water and topping up his glass.

If only, if only, if only I wasn't such a damaged man, he thought, as she brought the glass to his lips and held his head as he took a sip. If only I was a better man. He glanced at the pack. But I'm not, he accused himself guiltily.

Ruby set the jug down and leaned across him, her soft breasts brushing his forehead as she plumped up his cushions. As though satisfied she had finished her nursing duties, she wrapped herself in her favorite baby pink cashmere cardigan, drew up a chair and sat beside him.

"What the hell were you doing up the tree anyway?"

Interrogation time.

"Bird-watching," he growled petulantly.

"What possessed you to think you could fly through the canopy?" Ruby's eyes narrowed, "If I didn't know you better I'd say you threw yourself out of that tree deliberately."

"Now why would I do that?"

"You knew I'd be the only mug within miles who'd tend to your wounds. The only mug that doesn't know how to say no to you. The only mug that puts other people first. But I'm warning you Oliver Hart, don't make trouble. Carlos and I will get married one day and no amount of throwing yourself out of trees is going to change that."

Oliver scowled. Bloody Carlos. Would he ever be free of that man's shadow?

He pinched the ridge of his nose then swept his brow with his hand. His gaze drifted to Ruby. Did he owe her his life? He shuddered to think what would have happened if he had lain concussed for much longer.

Yet she was to blame as much as he was. He'd been thinking of her when he fell. His thoughts distracted by visions of her loveliness. Her perfect, unblemished skin. Her exquisite, flawless soul.

Her perfection was as enticing as it was dangerous. Would she flee when she discovered his deception?

He followed her every move as she left the room, her head of curls coiling like Medusa's serpents. Her sexy hips swaying like a temptress in her floor-length maxi dress.

She glided across the floor as if she knew he was watching but was pretending with confident assurance not to care.

Already she had proved distracting. Already his fascination had become obsessive. Already she had proved she could be dangerous. Next time would he be so lucky?

A roar like dull thunder quaked through his heart. There was no point in playing Mr. Macho. There was no point in resisting. If Ruby wanted to tend his wounds, who was he to complain? Hell, he grinned, this may even be pleasurable. He couldn't think of a sexier nurse.

~

RUBY DREW the sponge along his 6-pack abs, down across his navel, avoiding the tented pitch protruding proudly from his loins. She folded back the sheets with the professional discretion of a masseuse, anxious not to further excite her patient.

He winced as she gently dabbed Dettol over his wounds. It was as though his pain was her pain. His torn flesh her flesh. His vulnerable uncertainty, her own.

She noticed a suspiciously large gash over his left thigh then sighed with relief. Thank god the family jewels had been protected, she thought, suppressing a giggle.

Tentatively she continued bathing him, pressing her hands with clinical efficiency, pinning her fingers steadfastly to the sponge least flesh should touch his.

She suppressed a gasp as inevitably an errant finger strayed, like a wayward child testing the repercussions of its defiance. Bolts of pure electricity shafted through her.

She jolted her hand, escaping the heat, and plunged it into water least the electrical currents emitting from his taunt, muscular chest singe her resolve, torch her will, set fire to the desire she fought so hard to quell.

Succumbing once was a mistake. Twice would be unforgivable.

23

"IF YOU'RE GOING TO STAY HERE YOU MAY as well make yourself useful," Ruby said, thrusting a spade at Oliver. A week had passed, and he had shown with the determination of 100 oxen that he was not a man to be felled for long.

Keeping him occupied would keep him at bay and hopefully tire him out and, if his work ethic was as slack as her stepbrother's, put him off staying around any longer.

"What are we doing—searching for treasure?" he joked.

"You know, it's funny, when I look at my life I realize what a façade it all is. You've helped me see that," she said softly. "I've been so busy trying to please everyone else, nobody's even asked me what I want. But what infuriates me is that it's my fault for not standing up for myself."

"I'm glad you've come to your senses. You didn't answer my question," he said.

Ruby put down her spade and wiped the sweat from her brow. Would Oliver dismiss her ideas as Carlos and her family had? She decided to take the risk. She wanted him to know who she really was, how she felt, what shaped her, and what mattered. And to do that, she knew she had to allow herself to be vulnerable.

"My real parents abandoned me. I spent most of my childhood in foster care. At one of the places I stayed a white dove used to perch outside my window. Gradually, when I went into the garden it would come and sit with me. Eventually, it trusted me enough to eat out of my hand. It would look at me as though it really saw me." She turned to him uncertainly, warmth flooding her heart as she saw the genuine compassion in his eyes. "Just like the way you look at me sometimes . . . like you're looking at me now," she said softly.

"I know it sounds silly, but that dove always gave me hope. Hope that one day someone would love me enough to choose me, to commit to me, to say, 'yes, *we want you* and we're never going to let you go'. For better or worse the Diaz's gave me that security. But I never forgot the healing power of that bird. I want to give something back to kids who've lost hope, I want to show them the power of love."

She began to tell him about her vision for an animal sanctuary where kids and adolescents in need could receive therapeutic care, not just from the beautiful setting, but from the healing presence of horses, and cats, and dogs—even chickens,. She knew animals could instill love and affection to those starved of affection.

And she was pleased, elated, surprised even, when rather than dismiss her ideas as foolish, he encouraged her, revealing an unexpected depth of knowledge. She'd been right about his cats, Renshaw and Edwards. They weren't just reminders of independence and distrust, but symbols and reminders of affection and the healing power of unconditional love.

"Wouldn't you get lonely? No rockstars, money moguls, Fifth Avenue designer clothes to pretty yourself with?"

Ruby threw him a derisive look. "Not at all. I just feel like. . . I don't know. . . like my soul can breathe here. That this is where I belong."

"Right here?" Oliver raised an eyebrow as he contemplated the wild terrain where the Hope butterfly he coveted had made its home. "You continue to surprise me."

Ruby nodded. "I just feel it's where I'm meant to

be. If that means sacrifice on my part, it's a small price to pay."

~

SHE PICKED up the spade and plowed into the ground with a force that both surprised and excited him, deepening the respect and admiration he felt for her.

"You dig a deep hole for a slight wee thing," he said. "Planning on burying somebody?"

She grinned. "Maybe. Don't underestimate me, Oliver," she laughed, waving her spade at him.

Clearly, she wasn't the pretty wee bauble he'd mistaken her for. She was a strong woman, determined to make her way in the world independently —a trait he realized he both feared and respected.

"I'd better make myself useful lest I find myself on the wrong end of your spade," he joked, picking up a shovel and helping her dig.

"You know what I love about being out here? I love the more basic human interaction. It's so raw. So real. You're really connected to the earth and to the environment in a different way than how you are in the concrete mayhem of the city," she said, her face radiating with light. "I love being here, it's awesome."

She looked so happy, so peaceful, so beautiful,

Oliver contemplated, as she stood before him, devoid of make-up, her cheeks blushed with dirt, her hair a tangled mess, her teeny, weeny khaki shorts riding too far up those far too sexy buttocks as she bent over and picked up a small pile of dirt.

As the umber soil crumbled and fell between her fingers Oliver shuffled his feet. He ran his finger around his shirt collar. His feelings for her held him in a vice-like grip, squeezing his previously rock-solid conviction that his only motivation for taking her from Carlos was to rid her of a bad mistake and then, mission conquered, disappear out of her life.

How could he leave her when it meant going against everything he now valued? He picked up the rake at his feet and thrust it into the mound of freshly cleared dirt.

"Thank you for helping me, Oliver. For believing in me," she turned to him with those far too innocent, trusting eyes and Oliver felt his will power begin to crumble.

As he watched Ruby rip and tear scrub with her bare hands he knew with certainty only one beauty had the power to wrench the very fabric of the impenetrable life he had built. Only one beauty had the power to rip down the walls that had afforded him so much protection. Only one beauty could shower him with irreversible pain.

He grabbed a thistle bush and wrenched it from

the ground. Who was he kidding? He was raised in a world so glaringly opposite to hers. Nothing he could do would change that.

He'd be a permanent blight on the family tree, a tree the whole family were determined would never take root.

And yet, he brooded, staring toward the horizon, if he wrote a scientific paper documenting finding the rare and elusive Mexican Hope butterfly, and at the same time helped his sister find a cure for her crippling disease the international acclaim this would merit may just be enough of a point of difference to capture their attention.

He continued thrusting the shovel into the ground. He'd never be good enough for the Diaz's, he thought plunging it harder.

You want something, you take it.

Simple.

LOSS

It's so much darker when a light goes out than it would have been if it had never shone

~ John Steinbeck ~

24

"WHY DO I FEEL SO UNEASY?" A SINKING feeling pushed down on Ruby's stomach in a wave of nausea.

She stood up and walked to the window. She brushed the silk curtain aside gently and watched from above as the guests began to arrive.

The party had been called in her honor. Carlos had told her it was a belated welcome home. But he'd also once told her that he would never come back to 'this hell-hole.' None of it made sense.

And none of it quelled the shiver of unease that scuttled up her spine. She didn't like crowds and she hated being the center of attention even more.

Knots churned in her stomach as she gazed down at the guests carrying gifts, wrapped with large silk bows, and fine papers that glistened with threads of gold and silver.

It isn't my birthday, she thought anxiously, nibbling on her ringless fingers, as she returned to her dresser. She brushed her glossy curls, sliding the gorgeous diamond-encrusted butterfly clip in her hair. Dotted with sapphires and amethysts and edged in gold it had been couriered to her earlier in the day, accompanied only by an elegantly simple white card, embossed with the words, 'always in my heart.'

"May I come in?" Carlos pushed open the door and strode across the room, startling her from her thoughts.

"Of course, you needn't ask," Ruby said, getting up from her dressing table. Her eyes flew to the towering boxes he carried purposely in his arms which he placed decisively upon the bed.

"Thank you for the exquisite gift," she said, gesturing to the clip perched amongst her curls. "It's perfect."

A shadowed frown cast a grim dark line over his face.

"Open them," he said, ignoring her reference to the gift and pointing to the elegantly wrapped boxes littering the bed.

His gaze, she noted with discomfort, as he watched her walk toward the boxes majestically emblazoned with the French couture house's Dior logo, was analytical, appraising, calculating. It was as though in studying her curves, the gracefulness of her walk, the lean perfectly proportioned lines of her body, he was admiring her like a stud owner admires a filly he's preparing for show.

"It's a little something I picked up on our recent trip to Paris," he said, as she began to untie the large red satin bows.

Ruby smiled weakly. "You spoil me. You shouldn't have." She walked across to the bed, her stomach churning with a nervous energy which she found unsettling.

"I want you to look beautiful."

Ruby stiffened.

"Don't you like what I'm wearing?"

Carlos shrugged as he studied the clean, classical lines of her dress. "You are a beautiful woman. But your preference for understated elegance does not show you off to perfection. You could shine more, my darling, and then everyone would see what a truly lucky man I am."

Ruby smiled tightly. He didn't mean to be unkind but she couldn't help feeling like a show pony, about to be paraded for other people's pleasure.

She lifted the lid off the Dior box, unfolded the tissue and took out the dress Carlos had purchased for her.

"It's lovely," she said, trying to hide the overwhelming feeling that flooded her body.

"Put it on," he commanded, leaning against the wall, one arm folded over the other, his hand resting firmly under his chin.

She walked toward him. "Can you unzip me?" she said, turning her back toward him.

Carlos traced the back of her neck with his fingers, then unzipped her dress slowly, pausing briefly at the curve of her buttocks.

Ruby stepped forward quickly and allowed the elegantly simple Lanvin dress she had planned wearing to slip unceremoniously to the tiled floor. She gazed at the mound of crumpled silk wistfully.

She walked to the bed and put on the dress Carlos had chosen. She concentrated on maintaining an air of excitement. She smiled tightly, her mouth aching with the strain.

Overwhelming flurries of silk and lace, glittering with tiny rhinestones and lustrous with the glow of seed pearls swirled around her.

She felt surrounded, smothered, imprisoned.

"You look beautiful. Like a princess."

Ruby shifted on her feet. *I feel like an over-dressed meringue.*

"Now come, everyone will be wondering where we have got to."

"Carlos, you still haven't told me what's going

on. Are you celebrating something? Did you get the party nomination?"

"Not yet, but I am celebrating. *We are*," he corrected himself. "I've invited all our closest friends—even managed to bring in one or two surprises." His lips curved in a half-smile. "I hope you'll be pleased."

A wave of apprehension washed over her. She raised her hand and rubbed her temple, and swept her fingers over her head, unsettling the butterfly clip in her hair.

"Are you okay, my darling? You look pale."

"It's nothing. Just a slight headache, that's all."

"Nothing a good party won't cure, I hope," he said, impatiently. "Finish getting dressed and come and join your friends."

Her lips curved into a smile that didn't reach her eyes. My friends? Ruby gazed out the window again. She couldn't see a friendly face amongst them.

Acquaintances yes. Contacts of Carlos's, yes. Family, yes. But a true friend? No.

The crowd of celebrities, media moguls, entertainers, and politicians looked more like a meeting of who's who then people gathered to wish Ruby a heartfelt welcome home.

25

IGNORING A SHARP PREFERENCE TO RETREAT, Ruby emerged from the sanctuary of her bedroom and walked down to join the guests.

Despite her trepidation, she gasped at the stunning setting. Never had the garden looked so beautiful. Candles hung in crystal cases dripped from the trees lighting up the foliage like tiny glowworms.

A quartet played sensual melodies which drifted through the crowd. White-lined tables with crystal goblets and glistening silver peppered the lawn.

If she didn't feel so uncomfortable, so self-conscious, she would have inhaled the beauty of the scene and allowed her senses to succumb. But as she stepped amongst the gathering all eyes turned to her. The band ceased playing and a suffocating hush enveloped her as she wove her way through the strangers.

Her heart stopped, then beat rapidly. She felt like an actress on a stage playing a part she never wanted. The costume didn't fit. The actors were in the wrong play. Her life, this stage, was a farce.

Ruby froze. Her face paled. Her eyes widened like saucers. A nervous blush rose from her heart to her face.

Carlos stepped forward, placed an arm firmly around her. He pulled her close as though sensing her intention to flee.

He waved his free hand out across the gathered crowd, "This is a surprise for my beautiful Ruby, but not for you—you all know why you are here."

The guests laughed conspiratorially.

Ruby turned to Carlos, looked fleetingly back at the strangers, then returned her gaze to him, a nervous smile on her lips. Her mouth formed unspoken questions. Her eyes filled with bewilderment.

Suddenly Carlos bent down on his knee.

"Ruby, marry me."

It struck Ruby that it was a command as much as a proposal.

She froze.

Without waiting for her answer Carlos rose to his feet and took her hand. "This, my friends—" he said turning to the smiling crowd, as he slipped a gigantic diamond ring on her finger, "—is one of the most expensive engagement rings in history—and worth every dime."

A hundred gasps of appreciation mixed with envy permeated the warm, fragrant air.

"Don't hold everyone in suspense," Carlos whispered, "We're waiting for your answer."

She had no choice. Not now, not before. And yet she felt conflicted. It wasn't what she wanted, but how could she humiliate him in front of everyone that mattered to him? How could she say no?

"What's wrong, you don't seem happy," he said, leaning toward her, sweeping her cheek in the pretense of a kiss.

"Nothing," she whispered, "It's just, well I . . . I guess I always imagined a more private, more intimate engagement. Just the two of us."

"What and deny all these people a party? Silly thing," he said, dismissing her concerns.

"Ruby Diaz, will you marry me?" he repeated, turning to the crowd and waving his hands in the air in a deliberately overacted theatrical performance. But the playfulness in his voice conflicted with his steely gaze. The force of his grip as he turned toward her claimed her hand.

Ruby darted a hopeful glance into the audience. Hoping, beyond reason, that Oliver would come for her. Just like in the movies.

But it wasn't Hollywood. It was her life. Raw and real and full of responsibilities. Her parents were staring firmly at her, their smiles fixed with no trace of humor or amusement in their eyes, as she delayed.

The ring weighed heavily upon her finger, mirroring the heaviness in her heart.

For the briefest of moments, she imagined herself picking up her skirts and fleeing into the night; running from a fate which was not of her making; escaping from a future she knew now she didn't want.

Carlos's eyes blazed white fire, burning her fantasy, sending it plummeting to the earth like rocks spewing from a volcano.

"I will marry you, Carlos. *Of course.*"

He pressed his firm lips to hers as the deafening applause and cheers engulfed her.

"The ring came from the best diamond dealer in New York State, the House of Graff," he said, noticing her sadness, as though trying to reassure her that his wealth would change everything.

She gazed down at the fifteen-carat flawless emerald diamond set in a platinum jaw-dropping engagement ring.

"You look like someone's died," he said abruptly.

Ruby smiled tightly, reached up, and kissed his cheek.

"I'm sorry, truly. I guess I just feel a bit overwhelmed that so much fuss is being made of me. Now, who would you like me to meet?"

Carlos circulated introducing her to people whose faces she recognized from newspaper photographs, or television, and others whose titles or his brief description of their jobs indicated they would be helpful to her future husband's career.

Guests glittered with jewels and sparkly dresses under the garden lights. Some looked elegant, a few looked like they had tried too hard, but all seemed like they were having a good time

"Everyone who's anyone is here," she murmured once, as Carlos excused them both from one group and moved quickly toward another.

"Everyone who can boost my chances of nomination," he answered. "This is the perfect occasion to make sure that certain people see us in a certain light. The Diaz name still dazzles—and of course, your beauty helps."

Ruby bit down on her lip, suppressing a desire to tell him that she wished their engagement could have been a less public, less politically motivated affair.

"Now that we are engaged we will of course be spending more time in Washington."

Ruby's eyes widened. "Washington? But what about my dreams? What about *Casa Rosa*? I thought

. . . couldn't I commute? I could come and join you when you need me."

Carlos's eyes narrowed, he leaned in close to her, his voice low and stained with determination. "I need you, Ruby. Your place is with me. Your future is with me."

"But, I've already managed to raise some money through crowd-funding. I put a notice on Facebook —people are wanting to back me," she said breathlessly, "Carlos, this is important to me. There is so much need. So much to be done."

"My life is in politics. I need my wife to understand that. I need her to support that. You do see that, don't you? Take something else up as a hobby, just don't make it your career." He kissed her briskly on the top of her head.

"But Carlos, don't you see, it gives me purpose. It makes me happy."

"About children? About things that have no place in our life?"

Ruby's eyes blazed indignantly. "About making a difference. About sharing my experience. About helping others."

"No! I need you beside me, supporting me—as a good wife should."

Ruby searched his face for a sign. A sign that he was jesting. A sign that he did not mean to treat her as a possession, as an asset purely to further his career. Her heart sunk when she saw the resolve in his eyes and felt the steely determination of his arm as it wrapped around her.

"I cannot have my wife working. Not with the Senate elections looming so soon. That is final."

This is supposed to be the best day of my life, Ruby reasoned sadly, weaving her way through the crowd. Her breathing was rapid, her chest constricted. She needed space, fresh air, to escape, if but for a moment.

"I hear congratulations are in order," Oliver said, blocking her path.

Ruby sprung back, startled.

"My gift suits you," he said, gesturing to the butterfly clip in her hair.

"This was from you? You knew about Carlos's plans? He told you?"

Oliver could hear the hurt in her voice, he could taste the bitter unspoken accusation. 'Why didn't you stop him?'

He didn't know. All he knew was that he was here now, and it wasn't too late. "I have another gift," he said. "A flight." Of passion, he said silently, thinking that if she did not come willingly, he would take her.

"I can't," she said.

"You can. Carlos is going back to The States tomorrow."

"He is? He didn't mention it."

Oliver arched an eyebrow. "Do you talk to each other?"

"Of course we talk—it's just that . . ."

"It's just that tomorrow morning you'll be free to come flying with me."

Ruby looked back toward the party, her shoulders slumping as discordant voices buoyed by lavish amounts of alcohol twisted in the air. She turned back to him, her eyes glistening like stars. "Okay, why not."

"Good. Pack an overnight bag."

"No, Oliver, I can't do that. It will have to be a day trip. It wouldn't be right."

Fear clutched greedily at his innards. He felt like something precious was slipping away from him.

"A day trip it is," he said too quickly. Oliver hated lying to her; in fact, he was useless at it, but he couldn't see another way. He needed to have time with her alone, and a day trip wouldn't cut it. "But pack a change of clothes and some woman's stuff just in case the weather turns. One should always be prepared. We're heading for the mountains. You never know."

She regarded him dubiously, a frown on her delicate features.

"I don't know. Why do I get the feeling I can't trust you? Like you're up to something?"

"It's a surprise. Something I want to give you."

"You've already given me the perfect gift. Honestly, I love it."

Ruby lifted her hand to her hair and trailed her fingers over the butterfly clip. Her palm rested against it momentarily as though she was communing with it, asking the bejeweled creature whether or not she should deny him his wish.

When she spoke her voice had that husky quality that always excited his libido. "Just for the day, right?"

Relief fizzed in his blood. "Just for the day."

POSSESSION

To possess somebody is to destroy
all possibility of love

~ Osho ~

"WHEN ARE YOU GOING TO LET ME GO?"

Ruby demanded, pacing the polished tiled floor of the remote hillside retreat where Oliver had hidden her.

She should have looked happy surrounded by the vista of carefully tended gardens, filled with brilliantly hued flowers and towering ancient trees. Normally she would have noticed how the planting complemented the naturally lush, virgin, tropical landscape.

But Oliver knew now that it only reminded her of *Casa Rosa*, her home. The home he had abducted her from after her engagement was announced on the pretense of a celebratory flight of passion in his chopper.

"You can't keep me locked up here, cut off from the world forever."

Oliver scowled. Did she take him for a fool? He was fully aware he couldn't keep her closeted away from danger like the fragile butterflies he so zealously protected. No matter how much he wanted to.

Not like this. Not against her will. Not forever.

Oliver scanned the horizon, frowning as the thunderclouds moved rapidly across the morning sky.

"I'll be missed," she said, solemnly.

Oliver bit his bottom lip. *I'll miss you too—if I set you free.* He shifted his gaze from the approaching storm and turned slowly toward her.

"Do you really think letting you go will give you back your freedom?"

Ruby's brow knitted together. "I want to go home," she said softly.

Oliver shook his head slowly, "I'm doing this for you, Ruby. I saw how miserable you looked when he slipped on that ring. You'll thank me later."

Ruby's hands flew to her hips, "I'm not a butterfly, Oliver. I'm not some fragile, vulnerable creature you need to save from predators."

She marched toward him, her gaze unwavering. "I'm not someone you can capture, mount, pin, and preserve in some protected glasshouse. I can make my own choices, my own decisions—not yours!"

Oliver smiled wryly. He studied her meticulously, savoring the unique specimen that she was. Having fire in her belly suited her. "You're very hot when you get angry," he said playfully.

As he gazed upon her, it suddenly occurred how much she had come to mean to him. The way her cheeks flushed the prettiest shade of pink when she got mad. The clear shade of blue her eyes became when she was thundering home her point of view. The tenderness she had shown when she was nursing his wounds.

The brilliant intelligence, equally matched by a compassionate, generous heart, Ruby had revealed when she finally trusted him enough to share her dreams for the refuge for children. The impatient pout of her soft pink lips, now as she stood waiting for his response.

She was a keeper, but why was she always running away?

"You want to go. Fine." Oliver grabbed her by the hand more forcibly than he intended, and pulled her toward him violently. Her body yielded readily, unexpectedly warm and pliant. She fell against his heaving chest.

She looked up at him, their eyes met, glanced away, sought each other again. Was he mistaken or was that longing he saw indelibly printed in her eyes?

"I want to go home," she said softly, burying her face into his chest. "I'm needed." Her words tumbled hesitantly.

Oliver wanted to shake sense into her and roar, "I need you too. What about what I want? What we both want?" But pride, or was it ego, demanded she tell him she needed him first.

He set his jaw, irritated by the impossibility of it all. A large cloud shaded the sun, engulfing the room into dull, dank light.

"You need saving from yourself, Ruby. Always doing what others want, always letting others use you ..."

"Use me!" She pulled away from him and flew to the other side of the room. She spun around furiously. "The only reason you came back into my life was to get your precious butterfly," her voice quivered.

"You knew?"

"Yes, but not the way you think. I never rummaged around in that filthy pack of yours. Your sister contacted me."

"Jacqui?" Why? What possible reason would she have? Nothing was making sense. "Ruby, let me explain ..." Oliver walked toward her.

"Don't bother explaining. Jacqui told me. Did you really think so little of me? But that's not the point. The point is you still blame me, don't you? I know you think I betrayed your trust. But when my parents asked me about you all those years ago, I felt I had to be honest. So, yes, I told them about your past. I don't like secrets. Secrets always cover lies. So when they asked if the rumors they'd heard were true I told them about the things you had done. The time you'd spent as a teenager in a borstal because none of it mattered to me. I loved you. I knew you'd changed since then. I thought they'd understand like I understood. You were young. Angry. Hurt. Immature. I got that. *I still get that.*"

"Your parents still think I'm a pyromaniac. That I'll set fire to their precious name, burn the family heritage, blacken their fortunes. Okay, sure I was a little rash. But when I set fire to the toilet rolls I never thought the fire would spread and burn down the school gymnasium. And I never thought my parents would shun me either, leaving the state to issue corrective care. I did my time—and I paid the price," he said, the tempo of his voice slowing as though relieved to be finally expelling all the hurt of the past.

"But I never told you why. Now I want you to understand why I did the things I did and how this messed up fool never stopped loving you."

Avoiding his insistent gaze, she retreated as he approached. She sucked in a shallow gulp of air.

"This isn't love. Snatching me because you can't have what you want. Pretending it's for my own protection. I can't live like this—wondering where or how or when you'll take my freedom."

"You don't understand—"

"Don't . . ." she shook as he came closer, tears welled in her eyes. "I understand just fine. If you loved me you wouldn't have stayed away all these years. You've been trying so hard to be better than my family. And now you're trying to prove you're better than Carlos. Well, congratulations. You've won. You're their equal because you're just like them —motivated by possession. At least Carlos and my family are honest. Not lying and sneaking around behind my back."

Oliver grimaced. He hung his head momentarily before lifting his gaze to hers. "I'm sorry," he said softly. "You're right."

There, he'd said it. Finally said what he'd wanted to confess all along. Not just about the butterfly and his stupid bird-watching story, but his sorrow for all those years he'd stayed away. His sadness for all the things he should have said to her but didn't. His regret for all the times he should have been there for her but wasn't. And the fact that she had been right. Right to walk away from him all those years ago. Right to escape now.

But mostly he was sorry for the man he had become. There was no point explaining. How could she possibly understand when he didn't understand himself?

He only knew that just now, in this moment with the girl that meant the world to him, he'd seen his father and he hated how like him he had become. A cold, emotionally closed prick who'd thought he could control everything and everyone.

Even the woman he loved.

In a blinding flash of clarity Oliver vowed to do the thing he swore he would never do again.

"IF YOU LOVE SOMETHING, SOMEONE, YOU'VE got to set them free," Oliver affirmed quietly, as he reached into his pack.

"What are you doing?" Ruby's gaze flickered from his face to the butterfly as he took it from the glass jar and held it gently in his hands.

"I'm letting it go." He looked deep into her eyes, her wide gaze, and dilated pupils told him more than words ever could that she understood the magnitude of his decision.

She watched as he lifted the butterfly suspended between his thumb and forefinger in the air.

"But it means everything to you. What about the scientific article? What about the naming rights? What about completing your grandfather's collection? What about everything you've waited a lifetime for?"

she said quickly, the words tumbling into the charged atmosphere as rapidly as her heart was beating.

"None of that matters now. I have the meconium my sister needs—the other things, well I thought they mattered, but they don't. What's the point if I've got no one to share my passions with? What's the point if I have no heir to leave a legacy? What's the point of collecting more stuff to gather dust? Besides, I've always preferred seeing butterflies fly free. I'd like to think by letting her go she'll flourish."

"Let's go," Oliver carefully avoided her bewildered gaze and studied the fast-moving clouds. "Quickly before I change my mind."

Oliver strode across the room, threw open the door. The warm summer wind surged in enveloping him in sticky, humid heat. He ran his fingers around his collar. Everything felt so tight, so hot, so constricting.

The wind whipped through the trees, rustling the leaves, and bending the pliant branches back and forth. His own willpower ached to be bent too, as he waited for Ruby to gather her things and wait to be dispatched back to her life without him. But he stood firm.

He studied Ruby acutely aware that she was the reason for both his happiness and his sorrow. He'd never felt more torn and yet more certain. Could he really do it? Could he really change who he had be-come? He turned to her.

She stood in the doorway like an angel of light, the morning sun caught the gold highlights in her hair, sending them shimmering in a halo above her head. The wind flirted along the hem of her sheer cotton dress.

Ruby said nothing. She just stood there momen-tarily with sadness pooling in her eyes, and sorrow tugging at the corners of her lips as though saddled with unbearable regret. Her hands moved gently to her thighs, holding her skirt firm, as the wind stirred by Oliver's helicopter circled in a whirlpool of sultry, humid air.

His breath caught in his chest. God, she was beautiful. He clenched his fists and steeled his resolve.

"What are you waiting for?" he growled as he jumped into the pilot's seat. "Get a move on." He scanned the sky again. "The wind's not a problem now but it will be if you dilly-dally much longer," he cursed.

"I can't find my handbag," she called, her voice etched with worry.

"Get in," he commanded. "I'll get it. I know just where it is."

Ruby hesitated. It struck him she looked unusually worried. But he thought nothing more of it. Perhaps it was just nerves.

"Come on," he urged. "The way the wind is getting up, we can't afford to wait any longer. Not unless you fancy another night with me," he held his breath, hoping that she would give him the excuse he wanted to break his resolve.

He exhaled a disappointed sigh as Ruby came rushing toward him, ducking beneath the blades

"We both know that can't happen," she frowned as she took his outstretched hand, then allowed him to help her into the chopper. Her sweet scent filled the small cabin as she jumped into the passenger seat. Her soft smile temporarily thawed his solemn mood.

Did she have to be that thrilled about going?

"I'll go fetch your bag," he rasped.

Oliver raced back inside and searched the bedroom. Spying it partially hidden in the corner of the bedroom, he picked it up roughly. The contents spilled onto the floor. He scooped them up impatiently, threw a backward glance at the strange looking pen which had rolled under the bed. He left it and walked out of the room.

"Thanks—you're a life-saver," she said, clutching it as he handed it to her.

Oliver bit his bottom lip and fixed his gaze

firmly on the panel of instruments. Somehow he doubted it.

Ruby nestled into the leather seat and grinned. "It's just like being on The Bachelor," she said quietly, closing the door gently and turning to him.

"Yeah, but you didn't choose me did you?" he busied himself with the flight instruments as soon as the wayward words had spurted out.

Damn. If there was one thing he didn't plan to do it was wear his heart on his cotton sleeve. Not again. He steeled his resolve. Keep your mind on the task.

"Safety first," Oliver said, trying not to notice how her chest heaved and quivered.

He fought a heady desire to kiss her as he reached over and tightened her seatbelt. He swallowed hard as his gaze drifted from her breasts to her smooth flat stomach. He allowed himself to savor her long slinky limbs exposed by the thigh-high splits marching a line of seduction along her flimsy dress. Who knew when he would see her again.

He inhaled her scent again, growing momentarily intoxicated by her feminine odor, and basked in the warmth of her soft skin as his fingers brushed against her chest when he withdrew his arm.

Damn it, I can't help how I feel. His hands moved over her hungrily. Possessively. Ruby barely had time to resist. No chance to protest as his lips came down to take possession of her own. Strapped in her seat belt she did the only thing possible. She surrendered.

There was no attempt to warm her up with sensuality this time. No intention to beguile or seduce. His kiss was a powerhouse of passion, an offensive so sudden and so urgent that no defense could have been mounted, let alone sustained.

Strapped to her seat, imprisoned within the glass confines of the chopper, she had nowhere to go. He knew it. But he wanted to give her a kiss to remember. He knew they would never get another chance.

His mouth stormed hers, ravished it, eclipsing all thought with sensations that powered through his entire body, setting off adrenaline that stirred something deep and savagely primitive within him.

He quaked with the need to reach into her, stun and invade, to take and possess, to wreak as intensive a violation on her as that she was wreaking on him.

To his surprise and delight, she met his kiss with an explosive, sky-high passion that recognized only one pilot.

His hands moved to pleasure her lower body where he met with a desire that soared beyond his control. Ruby lifted her arms, wound them around his neck, twisted and arched her body.

A low growl issued, feeding on what he gave and took, greedy for each wild, unbridled foray of passion that fought for dominance that neither of them wanted to concede.

Searching fingers thrust through his silky mane, curled around his skull, and wrenched his head toward her.

A low exultant laugh graveled from Oliver's throat as Ruby stared up at him with glazed eyes. His gaze glittered over the curly tresses of her hair.

Frantically he ordered his mind to lift above the chaos of sensation that halted his willpower, eroded his reasoning, silenced his conscience.

The madness of his violent impatience to plunder the depths of her body stirred an equally insistent pride that demanded he do the right thing.

If they were to ever have any future it wasn't going to be like this, childlike quick, grasping, amateur, teenagers parked in a car.

"That was a mistake."

28

"OH." RUBY BLINKED. THAT SHE HADN'T expected. Her cheeks heated. She felt nauseous.

She looked up at Oliver as he expelled a whoosh of air from his lungs. His face, normally deeply tanned, was all shadows and contorted angles. He looked as awful as she felt.

The noise of the rotor drowned the silence that ballooned between them as they kept a reluctant distance. It was as if a treaty had been signed and ratified. There would be no more war.

As Oliver flew the helicopter through the air, deftly riding the currents like a bird, she should have felt wonderful. She'd just enjoyed the most sizzling, steamy helicopter kiss ever, she was flying high in a heaven-like sky with the man of her dreams at her side—yet she felt deflated. As though she'd got too close to the sun, too close to all that glittered brightly, too close to the person she knew sustained her life, and it had all melted.

She looked down, recognizing the giant metropolis of Mexico City—a crowded hotpot of color, but all she could see was funeral-gray. The helicopter was buffeted by a rough current and she felt her heart plummet to the ground, saw it about to shatter into a million pieces and felt powerless to stop it.

Her family needed her. She had made promises.

She turned and studied Oliver. His gaze locked ahead. How easily you can shut me out, she thought, reminding herself how unpredictable and self-serving he could be.

Yet here he was acting against his interests and taking her back. She didn't get it. It was so unlike him to concede defeat. Maybe he'd decided she just wasn't worth fighting for. He'd made his conquest, feasted upon her body, plundered her lips and now he would scan the terrain for the next elusive specimen to add to his bachelor collection.

She knew she was grabbing at straws. Talking herself into all the reasons Oliver was no good for her was meant to make the pain more bearable. Only it didn't. Because for every flaw he possessed, he had an equal, if not stronger, counterpoint.

He was successful, strong and normally persevering. She liked his intelligence, his resilience—especially his hard-earned street smarts—and the fact that he was spontaneous, fun, sensual and passionate.

Not just in the sack but passionate about his life. He had convictions that he would live and die for. Compared to Carlos, Oliver was positively colorful. He lit up her life.

But more than that, he had encouraged her to pursue her dreams. He had shared her conviction that her Eco Retreat was not just a winning one, but also a worthy one. And he had supported her unconditionally. His motive was never to own her but to free her from a bad mistake. And though it pained her to admit it, she knew he was right.

Ruby bit her bottom lip. She didn't know what she was going to do without him.

What to do? The choices were equally unpalatable. Marry Carlos and live the political life as an adoring wife permanently on show, encased in his campaigns. She would be no better than a mounted butterfly.

Or throw it all away—her impending marriage, her family land, and with it her family's love and acceptance. Could she really toss everything and risk a life of uncertainty with Oliver, when the last thing he wanted was to be tied down?

Ruby slumped in her seat. *If only someone or something would decide for me.* She yawned. Her mouth felt dry like it was filled with cotton wool. She suddenly felt overcome with fatigue. Her eyelids opened then fluttered shut.

She tried to sit upright in her seat but struggled to find the energy. Even keeping her eyes open was a challenge. Perhaps it was the stress of leaving, or that the highs and lows of the past few days were taking their toll.

But it was more. Much more and she realized almost too late. Ruby made a grab for her bag. She rummaged frantically through it.

It wasn't there.

She flung the bag on the floor, and kicked it open with her feet, spilling the contents.

She felt faint. Her eyes weren't quite open. She tried to speak. Her voice seeped from her parched lips, a quiet whisper, masking the fear she felt inside.

"Oliver, my insulin pen! Where is it?"

Ruby heard his anxious voice, his searching words, struggling to understand as she drifted in and out of consciousness.

She tried to hold on. To stay awake, alert, alive. But she felt tired, so tired.

A loud buzzing filled her head, she slumped against him and there was nothing but darkness.

29

UNABLE TO WAKE HER OLIVER DIALED emergency services. He described her symptoms over the phone. The twitching, the convulsions. He felt her pulse again—rapid like shooting pellets, studied her face—so pale, her body soaked in sweat.

The diagnosis was instant. "Severe hyperglycemia," the operator said. "It can be brought on by stress, or if a diabetic does not take insulin when required."

"Diabetic? Jesus. Why hadn't she said?"

"She should be taken to a hospital immediately, untreated it could lead to a diabetic coma or death."

Oliver checked the fuel gauge. He smashed his clenched fist on the dash.

"Stupid piece of shit!" he cursed. There was no

way he'd make it to a hospital. He checked his coordinates. Only eight minutes from the Diaz ranch. He prayed Ruby's family would be equipped to help. He phoned ahead to be sure.

Antonio ran to the chopper as it descended. He ducked beneath the twisting rotor and wrenched her seat buckle free.

Oliver killed the engine. Raced to his aid. They gently pulled Ruby's limp body free.

They stretchered her to safety, Oliver took her arms, Antonio her feet, and headed for the refuge of the house. Fear paralyzed Oliver's tongue. Oliver feared the worst, hoped for the best.

Joe Diaz glanced anxiously at his daughter, his eyes filled with a tenderness Oliver had never seen before.

Oliver wrung his hands helplessly. "I had no idea," he stammered, "She never told me." It made sense now, the sprinkle of needle marks on her stomach, her thighs, the back of her arms.

If she died it would be his fault.

Unspoken words of accusation and blame jackknifed through the air. Where the hell have you been and what have you done to my daughter?

Maria came bustling into the room, changing the angry mood with her calm, practical manner. She went to Ruby, felt her pulse, and turned to Antonio. "Get your father's insulin."

Joy was staring at Oliver with wildly accusing eyes. "You did this. If you hadn't filled her heart with flights of fantasy."

"Joy, stop it!" Joe hissed at her, his eyes stabbing a begging plea at Oliver. "She doesn't mean that."

Joy was too worked up, too distraught to listen to him. "You've always been bad luck. I knew something dreadful would happen. It was all a lie, wasn't it? You weren't here for Ruby. You were after something."

"Don't project your guilt on me, Mrs. Diaz," Oliver cut in, his voice shaking from his own overwhelmed sense of blame. "We're all at fault here."

Joy Diaz didn't even pause to take that in. The bitter accusing words kept spilling from her lips. "I knew it would come to no good. I knew it would never work. You snaked your way back here into her life, fooled her just to get back at us."

Oliver's control snapped. The exhaustive tension he had been under exploded in a passionate outpouring that finally silenced the woman.

"Who do you think you are?" he railed at Joy. "The world does not revolve around you, your land, your ambitions. You're so wrapped up in yourself and preserving your status you never once thought about Ruby's needs. You only thought about yourself."

"Oliver!" Joe Diaz hoarsely protested.

What had begun had to be finished. Oliver owed Ruby that.

"Do what you want with your life, play your political games, but find a new piece to play with, I'm not going to let you use Ruby as your marriage pawn." He flung at both of them.

"Ruby's life, her dreams, her desires are not yours to sacrifice. She doesn't belong to you. She doesn't belong to Carlos, she doesn't belong to me," he hesitated, took a deep breath, a huge lump swelled in his throat.

Now, holding Ruby's soft hair in his hand, feeling her faint pulse, he wondered what the hell he'd done. He had fought so hard to quell the powerful desire to claim her as his wife. What he had felt was too big, too deep, too raw and frightening. His regimen of hard work, discipline, self-denial had honed Oliver into a man of strength and single-mindedness to rule and conquer, not to lay his heart bare and succumb to neediness. The desire for safety wrestled with the need to open his heart and submit—to hell with whether they thought him worthy.

"I love her. I'd give up my life for her if I could. And so help me if—when," he corrected, fearing if he acknowledged his deepest fear it would manifest "—when she wakes up you'd better have given her back her freedom."

"Oliver . . ." Joe Diaz cut in urgently, then in a tone of despairing impatience, "Joy, for God's sake! For your daughter's sake, snap out of this! What more do you have to hear or see? What you're doing is destructive! It has always been destructive. You manipulate people until they're so screwed up they have nothing left to give."

"Joe?" Joy's voice trembled as the support she had depended on for so long eroded.

"Face it, Joy! For once in your life, face what you're doing, face what you've become and stop it!" he pleaded hoarsely.

"Can't you see? Oliver loves Ruby, and Ruby loves Oliver. *Oliver.* If Carlos loved Ruby he'd be here—not chasing his career. It has nothing to do with you or me or anyone else. Only them! And your anger is only making everything worse than it already is."

"But the wedding? The money? The land—"

"The land?" he let out an exasperated sigh and threw his arms in the air. "You ask about the land, yet you say nothing of Ruby. Can you not try to love her as your own flesh and blood?"

"Joe . . . don't. Not now." Maria cut in urgently, her eyes overflowing with despair.

He halted, clamped his mouth, then shook his head wearily. "I'm tired of this fighting, Joy. Tired of pretending to be someone I'm not. Tired of the lies," came his flat, weary retort.

"Deadly tired," he said, turning to face them all. "It's time Ruby knew the truth."

Joy's face blanched. Maria clutched her hands to her chest.

"This good woman, Oliver," Joe said, going to Maria's side, "Was my lover. She's Ruby's mother."

Oliver stood mutely silent, dredging up a shadow of a smile that threatened to crack the taut flesh of his face. How happy Ruby would be to know the woman who had loved her as a daughter was her birth mother. But the lies? How could he judge them? Hadn't he done the same thing—waited until it was almost too late to speak the truth that lay in his heart?

"I'm going to sit here quietly with Oliver. When Ruby wakes up I'm going to tell her the truth. Then I'm going to listen to the ideas she's been trying to share and I'm going to put all my energy into finding a way to help her. If you can set aside your jealousy, you'll help her too."

"Joe, I . . . I'm sorry."

"Sorry, without change doesn't cut it," he rasped. "This all happened before we met. If you can't let go of the past and be good-hearted, then go. It's one or the other. Is that clear? Just for once, you might think of someone else besides yourself!"

He took a few paces forward. His strong hand pressed on Maria's shoulder. "Is there anything we can do?"

She shook her head, too distressed to speak.

Joe turned to Oliver, "Oliver, there is no excuse I can give for my wife's behavior—I blame myself. It was so many years ago. My first wife had died. Maria was a great comfort . . . she never told me . . . she was ashamed . . . we weren't married—her family was religious," he gave an exasperated sigh. "She thought she was giving Ruby a better life. When I heard she sent our baby away, I did everything in my power to bring her home."

Oliver stared vacantly ahead. His head whirled. His chest constricted. His mind was an aching blank. He had no idea what was going on with Ruby's parents. All families have dramas, but right now all he cared about was the only woman he loved more than he had dared admit.

Maria's anguished scream ripped through the air, "Call an ambulance. Call nine-one-one. Hurry, hurry!" Maria laid her ear to Ruby's heart then began to press on it. "She's fading. Tell them to hurry!"

∼

"You know what kind of insect you are?" Oliver

said, reaching out to Ruby as she lay in the hospital bed three days after the incident. He gently lifted an errant coil of hair and tucked it behind her ear.

"Don't you dare say a bug," Ruby said.

"A bug? Hardly," his eyes glistened, "I was thinking more along the lines of a butterfly, a beautiful butterfly, the rarest gem of the insect world."

She knew she was in trouble again when he looked at her like that. "You've got to be kidding. I must look a washout—like a cabbage butterfly." She was a bug—an annoying bug that irritated everyone and everybody trampled. Not remotely like one of those nimble, colorful, pretty things with the freedom to transform themselves so effortlessly.

At least, that was what she had once thought. But she was getting stronger. Her illness had changed something. Had changed a lot, she corrected. She knew now that life was fleeting, happiness was fleeting—but even happily forever afters were fleeting she reminded herself as Oliver moved closer toward her.

"No I mean it," he said, his breath a rich chocolate caress across her cheeks. "If you were a butterfly you'd be an *Agrias hewitsonius beata* type. Exotic, beautiful, warm, vibrant, unique exceedingly rare."

She felt her face flush, her body shiver as he moved closer still. "They're flittery and fragile and delicate—and they take fright. "

"I don't take fright."

He took her hand in his and held it as though protecting what was his rightfully as she tried to pull away.

"I hadn't realized how much you'd come to mean to me."

The words slipped from his mouth so quickly, so unexpectedly, so honestly, Ruby responded without censuring her words. "You mean everything to me too."

No, not everything. He can't mean everything.

"I didn't mean that," she said.

"YES, YOU DID," he said softly. He stood and walked to the end of the room, bracing his arm against the open window. A soft breeze feathered across his chest and rippled his loose cotton trousers against his powerful thighs. But it did nothing to cool him. Even the plunge under a cold shower earlier hadn't brought relief from the turmoil simmering within.

He was the one so needy of love, but he was the one who couldn't settle. He should have silenced his fears, conquered his demons, abolished his parents and the Diaz's taunts that he was worthless. He should have done it eight years ago.

She'd listened to her parents then. He understood why. But she'd abandoned him. He knew it was irrational reasoning but when she'd nearly died he'd felt betrayed—as though she'd abandoned him again. As though, again, it was his fault. As though being loved wasn't his destiny.

Nearly losing her had been a cruel reminder of how fragile and painful his heart was. They'd had a second chance at love. Did her survival now count as a third? How many other chances would they have before he'd finally commit his heart and soul again and reclaim his lost love?

"Ruby!" he said, striding toward the bed. "I wanted to ask you . . ."

"What?"

"Did you ever love me?" It came out as a growl because inevitably his gaze had dropped again to where her hospital gown had splayed open revealing the creamy swell of her breasts.

When she didn't respond immediately he looked up to see her biting her lip.

"Yes," she said, softly. Her gaze settled on his chest, then swung to his eyes.

"I never stopped loving you."

LOVE

In the end, love wins. It does win.
We know it wins.

~ J.K. Rowling ~

30

F ROM ALMOST THE FIRST MOMENT SHE HAD seen him her life had no longer been her own, and now she simply couldn't comprehend living without him. In the last few months, during her fleeting visits back to New York he had proven that he hadn't wanted her just for sex. He hadn't admired her purely for her beauty. He hadn't wanted her to hang off his arm like a prized jewel.

It was more, much more than that. Ruby was certain of it now. Distance and time had given her clarity. When Oliver had abducted her he had said he wanted her at his side for the rest of her life, and he had surely meant it. His words and actions before and after her illness confirmed that beyond a doubt.

Ruby winced as she realized the terrible hurt she had given him in suggesting they be lovers. *Nothing more.* She hadn't meant that their relationship had to end, but now she understood why Oliver had reacted so violently.

To have offered his heart to her and then seemingly be told he was wanted as a short-term lover—the insult to his pride had been deeply wounding. Especially when months earlier, fearing he had lost her forever, he had pledged his love.

But slipping into a coma and facing death, and then hearing that everything she believed about her parents had been a lie, that Maria was her real mother, had instilled in her the knowledge that she needed some time alone to work out who she really was.

And she knew a big part of finding her essence was to stand on her own two feet and pursue her dreams independently.

Could she truthfully and confidently give Oliver the commitment he said he wanted when she had spent her whole life trying to live up to other people's expectations, fitting into their lives, sacrificing her dreams?

She wasn't ready, common sense insisted. But her heart kept urging that it didn't matter where their relationship was heading, or what heartache the future had in store for them, she could not turn her back on it, nor choose any other path.

She wanted to be with Oliver more that she wanted anything, and somehow she had to work everything else out first so that she could be true to herself. She was grateful too, for all that he'd done for her family. Taking her stepbrother aside, helping Antonio through the gambling addiction that had all but eroded the family finances. He even gave him a job so that he could service the mortgage Oliver's company had advanced him, and repay the debts he had wrongly loaded onto *Casa Rosa* and the surrounding land. Ruby had demanded it be that way —she didn't want Oliver's charity.

So much had changed since her health crisis. And it all centered around the Hope butterfly. Jacqui's symptoms had disappeared—technically she was in remission—but it looked promising. So much so that Jacqui decided not to put off her dreams anymore either. She had packed up her life in New Zealand in favor of devoting her life to finding natural remedies and helping Ruby provide medical care for the children who would come to the retreat.

And then there was Carlos.

Ruby was forcibly jolted back to reality with the limousine's arrival at the swanky hotel Carlos had insisted he pay for in New York. A glance at her watch told her that she barely had time to shower and change before their dinner date.

It was difficult to wrench her mind off Oliver as she soaped her body under the shower. Just the memory of that wild act of intimacy Oliver and she had just shared was enough to stir involuntary spasms of pleasure.

She even hoped that Carlos's talk to the investors she'd secured had been so wildly successful that her departure from New York could be delayed as long as possible. Just so she could spend more time with Oliver and his crazy cats.

That was being totally selfish, she chided herself. The staff back in Mexico would grow anxious if she delayed too long. There was still so much to do.

And Carlos wouldn't appreciate that attitude either, particularly since he had gone to the trouble of involving himself on her behalf. Ruby tried to get herself into a more responsible frame of mind, but even by the time she was dressed and presentable, her thoughts were still fluttering around Oliver.

The knock on the door brought her thumping down to earth. She took a deep breath. In the past few months Carlos had changed. He was a man she liked and admired and respected, and he deserved her full attention. And her gratitude. She opened the door and smiled a welcome.

He was dressed in a beautifully tailored, dark

gray suit and looked every inch a man of political power; handsome, distinguished, impressive, a man of strong character and deep convictions.

Few women could fail to appreciate so many attractive qualities, and he carried an individuality that successfully crossed all socio-economic barriers.

"You look positively radiant, Ruby," he said approvingly. "I'm happy to see that your near-death experience has not caused you any lasting trauma."

Ruby's heart danced an exultant jig at the thought of admitting the truth. A new zest for life was leaping through her veins, but it was because she ended their engagement and had gone to Oliver, not escaped him. And she knew that ending their relationship had lifted a great burden of responsibility from Carlos too.

Of course, quite possibly his change of heart was more to do with how quickly he rebounded in the arms of Lucinda Perez, the daughter of a wealthy oil magnate. Not only was she rich and well connected, but she was also extremely jealous and possessive.

An excellent match, Ruby thought, with not a small amount of pleasure.

"Come in, Carlos," she said quickly, swinging the door wide open and waving an invitation for him to enter.

He hesitated, then gestured down the hallway.

"What's wrong?" she asked with startling intensity.

He crossed the space between them with a couple of strides and took Ruby's hands in a grip that was strong and rough and urgent.

"I want you to have something."

Ruby was dumbfounded by his sudden change of manner. Grim purpose was stamped on his face, and the steely glint in his eyes warned that he would not be diverted from his purpose.

"Carlos?" It was a tense reminder that he hadn't answered her.

"This belongs to you," he said, as several men entered the room carrying a large parcel wrapped in brown paper.

"What?" Shock and conflicting emotions chased across her face, as she tore at the wrapping, knowing instinctively the treasure that lay beneath.

Butterfly Lovers.

"Why?"

He withdrew from her both mentally and emotionally, searching, struggling for answers that he could try and fit together himself.

"I didn't love you. I never did," he said pointedly, watching to see what impact his naked words had on her. "And I don't deserve this painting. It's yours. Yours and Oliver's. It always was. Lucinda wants you … *we* want you," he corrected, "to have it back."

He suddenly broke into a torrent of voluble Spanish, which was almost too fast for Ruby to fully comprehend. When at last he stopped apologizing for his behavior, he turned to her and simply said, "You deserve to be happy."

With slow, careful deliberation, Ruby set about clearing the path. "Thank you for giving me this gift —and thank Lucinda too. And thank you for everything you have done. For making it easy. I had no one to turn to before, but I do now. I have you as my friend and Oliver as my lover."

"His love is real, Ruby. It's one of those forever kinds of love. He told me that."

31

WOULD SHE REJECT HIM? BEADS OF SWEAT nestled on his brow as he climbed out of the Land Rover and headed toward Ruby's Mexican retreat.

This is crazy. Oliver reminded himself he'd been in situations far more terrifying. Situations where he could have died. She's just a girl.

He shook the tension from his arms, futilely attempting to relax. The worry burst through defiantly.

She's not just any girl, is she, Oliver? She's the one. The girl he loved and wanted to spend the rest of his life with. He knew with diamond-like clarity Ruby made life worth living. That his life had meaning and purpose as long as she was in it.

His emotions ricocheted with panic. What if she said no again? Why should she say yes? He'd set her free, ceded to her request they remain lovers, lied to her that commitment still felt like a ball and chain, made it clear that he valued his independence as much, if not more, than she did.

All for her own good. He shook his head at the irony of it all. He'd been more successful with the ladies when he was self-centered. But he'd changed.

He used to think achievement came from possessing what others coveted. He now realized that you may be able to own something but you can never own someone—especially the woman you love.

But that didn't mean you still didn't have to fight for it.

Like a flower suddenly freed from the shadow of a massive tree she'd flourished in her independence. Freedom and self-reliance had fertilized her soul.

He looked around with pride at what she'd achieved. *La Pasión de Paraiso*—the sanctuary of her dreams. The sanctuary she had persisted with despite formidable obstacles. The sanctuary she had built in spite of the cynics.

Pride fanned the coals of his soul. Ruby Diaz had become a strong woman. A woman to be respected. A woman to be admired. A woman to be loved.

Oliver's heart fluttered as she emerged through the clearing beyond the tropical forest. The sun filtered through the trees, bathing her in a halo of golden light. Her face glowed with a radiance he had never seen. She was exquisite.

He inhaled the comforting pristine air deep into the crevasses of his lungs. He clenched and unclenched his hands, forcing himself to stop visualizing the worst.

She didn't need him now. She was free to do as she wished. Would she want him? Choose him? Reject him again? What the hell, he reassured himself. It was worth the risk.

A spontaneous smile washed over her face, as she greeted him. His shoulders dropped with relief. He took her hand and led her down the winding pebbled path that led to the special spot he had prepared.

He looked up at the cloudless sky and hoped his dreams and meticulous planning provided her with an exceptional experience.

He heard them before he saw them. Millions of monarch butterflies beating their tiny wings filling the air with a sound like a shower of rain.

He turned to Ruby as she witnessed the unique

phenomenon, and in her delight he saw his future. The shadow of loneliness that had haunted him all his life lifted, leaving a feeling of peace as soft and serene as the butterflies raining upon them like confetti.

Ruby met his gaze, smiled tentatively, then turned and lifted her face, her eyes sparkling with excitement as the dazzling creatures fluttered around them, accomplished dancers in nature's most phenomenal, magical show.

The sweet smell of frangipani trailed after the butterflies as they clustered in small areas of the forest reserve, coloring the giant fir trees orange and literally bending their branches under their collective weight.

Fighting his nerves, he took her fidgeting hand in his, placed it gently on his chest, and pressed her palm to his heart as it raced. "Can you feel what I feel?"

Ruby bit her lip, looked down and studied the wildflowers pushing up beneath her feet.

He placed his fingers gently under her chin, raised her face to his. "Ruby, you've captured my heart."

Her lips quivered, "Please, Oliver before you say something you'll regret . . ."

"The only regret I'll ever have is not fighting for

your love. For not having allowed myself to love you sooner," the words he'd been waiting a lifetime to say suddenly became easier. He bent down on one knee and withdrew the gold silk box from his pocket. "I love you. Will you marry me?"

The sense of release was exhilarating. Those seven words he'd had the courage and conviction to finally say unburdening him from his storehouse of carefully repressed emotions. The fear of commitment, the fear of abandonment, the destructive need to prove himself, again and again, scrambling free, releasing him from his psychic cell that had kept his heart imprisoned.

"Oliver, I have something to tell you . . ." she hesitated, cleared her throat and avoided his searching gaze, "there's someone else."

Oliver stared at her in blank shock, the stab to his heart as fatal as a stingray's barb.

"I should have told you, but I was afraid . . . afraid of this. I knew you'd do something heroic," she stammered as her gaze swept over everything he had prepared, affirming with regret the effort he had made to ensure the most romantic of settings. Not just the butterflies, but the virgin beach covered with beautiful shells, the trees strung with silk ribbons, the rose petals sprinkled under a table dressed in antique embossed cotton, wrapped in a vibrant orange bow, her favorite color. And the table covered with the most exquisite food, champagne chilling—she noticed it all.

You name it, it was there. Romance to the max. But he was too late.

32

A S A GIRL SHE HAD DREAMED OF AN ALL-consuming love and a romantic proposal under a starry sky. But this was way better than anything she could have possibly conceived.

Tears welled in Ruby's eyes. It would have been perfect, any girl's dream. And it didn't escape her that the intimacy of the setting was so significantly different from the day Carlos proposed. She shuddered as she recalled the horribleness of that.

As though fighting his emotions Oliver took her hand. He held her fingers in his. "No matter what you say, Ruby, I won't accept no. Not anymore. I can't, I won't stop loving you, but from now on I want you as my wife. And no one will come between us."

He caressed her thumb with his. "We can work it out. We've come through so much. Please don't give up on us now."

Ruby's lips trembled. She pressed them firmly, closed her eyes slowly, and shook her head softly from side to side.

She didn't want him to marry her because he felt he had to. She didn't want to be rescued. She wanted to be loved. Accepted for who she was and who she had become.

She had stood up to her parents. Told them she loved them but things were changing. From now on she would make the decisions in her life.

They may not approve of Oliver, she had said. He may be from the wrong side of the Hudson. He may be trouble. But he was her trouble. And she wanted his kind of trouble bad.

She glided her hand over the firm little mound beginning to protrude beneath the cotton smock covering her stomach. The irony struck hard. She'd have to face them now.

"We're having a baby," she said, her voice taut. His reaction, however, took her by surprise.

He stared at her in blank shock. "What did you say?" he demanded, his voice slightly choked.

"We're having a child," she repeated unsteadily. "I thought you knew. Isn't that why you came?"

"You mean . . . you're pregnant? Now?"

"Yes," she said, barely able to contain her delight. So he hadn't come out of a sense of duty. "I thought I might lose the baby, I was told I'd never conceive . . . that's why I haven't traveled, why I've been so distant, why I never told you. Jacqui's been working at the clinic, helping with the kids and researching natural remedies. But you knew that. I thought she must have called you."

"Nope. Not a word."

Ruby was relieved that rather than be angry, his mouth curled in a hungry smile that made her breath fly. He dropped to his knees, pressed his lips to her belly, and peppered their growing baby with butterfly kisses. She felt her pulse riot in response.

As though sensing the magic that danced between them the butterflies drifted forward in a magnificent cloud. As Oliver rose to his feet, and wrapped his arms around her, they encircled them, weaving between them, and dancing around their heads.

Oliver leaned over and touched his lips to hers and she sighed into the kiss she knew would last a lifetime. And now she was certain they both really understood what true love was.

It was heaven. Pure heaven.

EPILOGUE

OLIVER AND RUBY'S BABY DAUGHTER WAS born the following Spring—they named her Jacqui Maria.

Joe and Maria married as soon as Joe's divorce became final. And they became the proudest grandparents in Mexico.

* * *

FLIGHT OF PASSION is now available as an audiobook for your listening enjoyment. Check out a free sample or grab your copy from your favorite online retailer.

THANK YOU

Thank you for reading *Flight of Passion*... I hope you loved it. If you did...

1. Help other people find this book by writing a review
2. Signup for my new releases email to find out about the next book as soon as I release it, sign up here http://eepurl.com/ghM501
3. Email me at mollie@molliemathews.com with a copy of your honest review and let me know if you'd love to join my dream team and of advance readers
4. Follow me on BookBub, https://www.bookbub.com/authors/mollie-mathews

5. Stay in touch on Facebook, https://www.facebook.com/molliemathewsnz
6. Follow me on Twitter - https://twitter.com/Molliemathewsnz
7. Be inspired on Pinterest - https://nz.pinterest.com/molliemathews and Instagram - https://www.instagram.com/molliemathewsauthor
8. Follow my blog - https://molliemathews.wordpress.com

Keep reading for a preview of the second book in the True Love series, Claimed *by The Sheikh.* (available in paperback and eBook)

ACKNOWLEDGMENTS

I'm very blessed with some wonderful cheerleaders and writing friends. Amongst those instrumental in bringing *Flight of Passion* to life are the wonderful people who offered to be beta readers. Having your feedback and sharing in the joy, and challenges, of bringing a beautiful book into the world made all the difference in finishing and publishing this book.

Thank you Coralie Unwin for your fabulous editing.

And to the love of my life—Lorenzo, my Templar Knight. Thank you for believing in me. Without your support, commitment, inspiration, and love of butterflies, I could never have written this book.

AND FINALLY...

Thank you for purchasing and reading my books. You are more than my livelihood—you let me live my passion. Without your love of romance and belief in the power of love, this book would never have been born. I really hope you loved *Flight of Passion* book as much as I enjoyed writing it. Here's to an extraordinary level of love and happiness in all our lives.

With love,

Keep reading for an excerpt from

Claimed by The Sheikh
Book Two in the True Love series.
By Mollie Mathews

Now available from Blue Orchid Publishing

Claimed
By The Sheikh
MOLLIE
MATHEWS

CLAIMED BY THE SHEIKH

THE SHEIKHS UNTAMED BRIDES

MOLLIE MATHEWS

CLAIMED BY THE SHEIKH

BOOK TWO IN THE TRUE LOVE SERIES.

Available now

A grief-stricken Sheikh Tariq na Hassir, the formidable ruler of the Kingdom of Avana, arrives in

Paris to claim his brother's child after a car crash killed his parents--only to find out from the hospital that the child isn't their biological son. It's Tariq's son, with his former lover.

Three years ago, after being banished by Tariq from his desert kingdom, renown architect Melanie Jones secretly gave her baby to Tariq's childless brother and his wife, in a swap the world was never supposed to discover.

The tragedy pulls her back to the world that rejected her and the man who abandoned her—the only man capable of tuning her carefully controlled world upside down.

Tariq will do whatever it takes to protect his legacy, including claiming Melanie as his bride and his son as heir before scandals ensue. But Melanie has other plans for her future—a westernized life where she's free to operate her own business and control her own life.

~

Join Mollie's new release newsletter here http://eepurl.com/cigEsH. Be the first to know when *the next book in the series* is released.

NOTE FROM THE AUTHOR

Dear Friends,

I hope you enjoy *Claimed by the Sheikh*. It touches on a number of subjects I love and care about with the twists and turns in the plot. I always love celebrating the strength of the human spirit, and what people do when faced with seemingly insurmountable challenges in their lives, and how unexpected events can turn disaster or tragedy into something good.

I love the fact that Melanie follows an unusual path as a pioneering architect. I love how hard she works at it. I always enjoy exploring how each of us uses and expresses our particular talents. And I felt a bond with her because I too studied architecture —but I didn't have the courage and determination that Melanie had to finish.

Watching Melanie struggle with discrimination, knock-backs, and success, and the price you pay for them, was familiar to me too. Each person lives success differently and her adventures along the way help her become the person she is destined to be. Whatever your path in life, you have a gift. Something nobody else can do as beautifully and skillfully as you.

How you express it, how you live it, and how you share it with others is unique to you. You have your own special way of dealing with life and the talents you've been given, whether you hide those gifts or share them openly.

I hope you enjoy reading about this talented young architect, and following her story as it unfolds. Victory and success come in many forms and guises, her path is an exciting, fascinating, and rewarding one, and I'm sure yours will be too!

With all my love,
Mollie

held my interest from the first page to the last. The story had a depth to the characters and strong imagery due to the author's attention to details. Watching two worlds collide, as well as two strong characters fight for what they each believe is right, just added another layer to the story.

I enjoy books that are set in the desert with desert royalty or sheikhs. Claimed by the Sheikh was a strong story with a depth to the characters of both Tariq and Melanie who we get to know a little at a time as well as their history from three years before. They seem to have unresolved issues and feelings for each other but given their differences will it be any different this time around? There was very strong imagery due to the vivid descriptions of the scenery, the palace and Melanie's drawings, which made me feel that I was there. Tariq's rescue of endangered animals and his philanthropy was a nice addition to the story. I liked how the child, Salim, was brought into the story as well as his importance to the storyline. Ms. Mathews is fast becoming a favorite author."

~ JoAnne

"This book grabbed me from the first page. Both lead characters were portrayed fully as real people not just by how they looked as in many books. There being a child involved added to my enjoyment!"

~ **Melba**

"The tone for this book is set in the opening chapters as the young Sheikh is faced with ongoing difficulties in the kingdom created by his atrocious father. He is fighting an ongoing battle to prevent himself from being sucked into the past and to rather create a new and prosperous future for his people. Tariq's previous rejection of Melanie and the results have soured her against romantic love and made her determined to carve a career for herself. "

~ **Margaret**

"I really like the premise of the book, I always like the royal romance with impediments to happiness and this book has it in spades. I like the strong figure of the Sheikh and the strong heroine who has built a professional career. Immediately I can see lots of problems that seem insurmountable at first: their past stormy relationship, the baby secret, her desire to have her own career, his desire for an heir, his demand to raise the child, his vow to swear off women. I also like that, right of the bat, we learn about his plan to build a reserve for animals and to right the many wrongs from his father's legacy. These are all good foundations for a fiery, passionate and conflicting relationship."

~ Elaine

"Fantastic premise that has a substantial conflict behind it. I like Melanie a lot. A strong female heroine is what I want to read. I think that is particularly important with such a powerful man, and here in this instance, someone who can wield such power. I love love love the beginning. This is one tough guy but the book opens with him protecting a baby giraffe. Fantastic opening."

~Leanne

"Tariq's emotional conflict is that he is in love with Melanie and won't admit it to himself. As a reader, it keeps me on pins and needles to see if Tariq realizes it himself."

~ Tonni

"It hooked me, it was impactful and well written.

Sexual tension is always a plus for me and I loved the strong characters."

~ **Terry**

"I wanted to keep reading. It was intriguing."

~**Robyn**

"Claimed by the Sheikh has an intriguing plot: keeping the Sheikh's illegitimate child a secret through all the complications that arise. The main characters, Melanie as the independent architect and Tariq as the wealthy, powerful Sheikh of a fictitious Arab country are well fleshed out and believable. You have empathy for their situation and the tension about whether the secrets will be revealed carries you through the book. This is the stuff of fairy tales. The book does go a long way towards helping the reader understand Tariq's Islamic beliefs and his commitment to helping his people and the endangered animals he wants to rescue. There is a nice subplot about Melanie's struggle to become recognized as a creative architect in a field dominated by men. Tariq's wealth comes in handy there. A good heartfelt romance."

~**Elaine**

The traffic on the motorway started to speed up as they got closer to Charlotte's husband's new office in the French headquarters of the Fédération Internationale de Football Association in southern France.

Salim was still asleep in the backseat when Charlie looked at her watch and realized it was nearly 1 am and they were going to be late to pick up Zayed. If he was exhausted, as he often was at the end of a long day, she knew he wouldn't wait. He had been working so hard rebuilding his life to provide for her and Salim. Tonight had been a special celebration. She was proud that he had won the election to be the new FIFA president. His campaign focused on change, football ideals and uniting warring countries through their common passion for sport. She didn't want to be late.

Charlie grabbed her iPhone from the dashboard and placed it in her lap, to send him a text, when Salim suddenly woke.

"Don't drive and text, Mommy!" he said, disapprovingly. "You'll cause an accident."

"I just want to tell Daddy that we're running a few minutes late, but we're almost there. Otherwise, he'll grab a ride with one of his staff and leave before we arrive." Charlie looked down and started texting quickly, holding the steering wheel firm with one hand.

Ten minutes later Salim saw his father first as they approached the building where he worked. "Daddy!"

Charlie pulled to the curb, got out of the car and opened the passenger door. Salim had already unbuckled his seatbelt and climbed out of his booster seat. He ran to his father.

Zayed scooped him into his powerful arms and drew Charlie to his side. His sheer strength and physicality always made her swoon and she leaned into his chest.

"*Marhabaan, habibti*. Hello, my love. How's my favorite team?" he said, placing a kiss on Charlie's lips before turning to Salim and kissing his chubby cheeks.

"You must be tired," Charlie said.

Zayed heaved a deep breath, sucking the early morning air into his lungs. "Exhausted!"

"I'll drive," Charlie said. "Why don't you sit in the back and take a nap? I don't want you to be too tired to give me some special attention when we get home," she laughed, planting a sloppy kiss on his sexy lips.

She was thinking about Melanie and how grateful she was to her sister as she embraced Salim and Zayed. She wanted to take a selfie of them and send her a text but they agreed not to stay in contact. Those were the rules. Besides they had their own busy lives in separate worlds. She wasn't obliged to call, but she wanted to. But she didn't want to upset her or retraumatize her sister either. It wouldn't be fair to her. Not when Charlie was so happy, and Melanie was all alone. *Without Salim.*

Charlie swallowed back the little trace of guilt that she never managed to kick and smiled as she watched Zayed clamber into the car, curling his long-powerful frame like a contortionist, into the back. He waited for Salim to climb in and rested his head against the booster seat and fell asleep.

She was so happy. She didn't need to be a princess. She didn't need Zayed's royal title. All she needed was her two favorite men, she thought as she pressed the keyless start and pulled out from the curb.

Charlie wanted to get home quickly. Both her boys needed to be in their beds. She hadn't wanted to leave Salim with a babysitter and was feeling a little reprehensible for lifting him from his warm bed to pick up his dad, but she knew how much Zayed had missed them both. He had been working so hard and tonight had been a well-earned celebration. Thankfully their home was only a fast 40 minute trip on the A7 autoroutes du Soleil.

They hadn't traveled far when Salim's eyes suddenly fluttered open. "You're not wearing your seatbelt!" he censured.

Charlie glanced at him in the rear-view mirror and noticed that Salim and Zayed weren't buckled in either. She'd heard the chime but had been distracted, worrying about Melanie, and how she must be suffering. She'd been rushed and stressed all day.

"Neither are you," Charlie said, turning around.

"I forgot, mommy," Salim said, he rubbed his sleepy eyes and started to put his seatbelt on, but it was caught in the door and he couldn't. He tugged and pulled on it. "It's stuck, mommy."

Charlie's heart raced as she turned to keep her eyes on the road. She was sitting right on the legal speed limit of 80 mph. It always felt so fast. Behind and in front of her was a line of other cars and there was no room to pull over. She couldn't stop now, without causing an accident.

"We'll be home in a minute, darling," she said, glancing at Salim again in the rearview mirror. The words had barely left her mouth when his eyes flew wide in horror. He saw a huge tourist bus careering toward them from the left.

PROLOGUE (CONT.)

Salim screamed. Charlie turned too late. The bus hit them with monstrous force.

Zayed woke and hurled his body across his son instinctively.

There was the sound of crushing metal and splintering glass as Charlie's cellphone flew from her hand. Salim watched in horror as his mother shot through the windshield like a torpedo. She careered through the air and disappeared under the cars in front. Their SUV struck another, stopped abruptly, and Salim and his father were crushed amongst a mangled heap of other cars.

The bus had shunted them three lanes over. The driver lay motionless with his head on the steering wheel as people rushed from their cars toward him, and several others ran toward Charlie's car.

The sky was ablaze with tiny lights from their cellphones as people were calling the emergency services. A crowd was staring at Charlie under the vehicle where she had landed, covered with blood and broken glass. Traffic was backed up behind them, and within minutes sirens screamed in the distance. People wandered dazed and numb with shock as they surveyed the carnage.

The driver of the bus was concussed and staggered from the wreck, but there was no sign of life under the car where Charlie had landed. Salim lay beneath his father's powerful body, his head, face, and arms covered with blood. No one dared touch Salim or Zayed for fear of injuring them further. No one knew if they were alive. As they waited for the emergency services to arrive it looked hopeless. But there was so much blood and twisted metal everywhere, no one could see clearly.

A paramedic team arrived by helicopter. The crew pulled Salim and Zayed from the wreckage.

Zayed was pronounced dead and Salim was immediately assessed as in a critical condition. They inserted a breathing tube before they left the scene and airlifted him to a hospital in Montpellier with life-threatening head injuries. More paramedics and emergency services arrived, including an ambulance, sirens shrieking and lights flashing,

They removed Charlie and Zayed's body from

the scene. It was hours before traffic began, moving again. In total, two people were dead, and eight people had been injured but none severely except Salim. The police and paramedics had said Zayed had died instantly when his skull was crushed against the hard surface of the television in the backseat of the car. When Charlie was thrown through the windshield and hit the pavement, she had died on impact. It was a tragedy made less horrific by knowing death had come instantly and they hadn't suffered.

The police found a blue backpack with an image of Simba from the movie The Lion King, and a soft toy of Simba too, on the floor of the car. The backpack had a name badge with Salim's name on it, and Charlie's purse with her driver's license was crushed in the front passenger seat, together with her cellphone. The screen was shattered but they could still see the picture of Charlie, Zayed, and Salim smiling on the home-screen.

Charlie and Zayed were taken to the morgue by the police. There was nothing in Charlie's purse or Zayed's wallet listing next of kin or who to notify in an accident. All they knew, for now, were their names and that they weren't French.

The paramedics had assessed that Salim had a serious head injury, a broken arm, and probably internal injuries. The police noted that none of them had been wearing seatbelts. All the police could deduce was that Charlie hadn't seen the oncoming bus, and possibly had been on her cellphone or texting. Both were common causes of accidents and fatalities. Beyond that, they knew nothing not even whether Salim would survive the accident. It looked unlikely when they'd left the scene and flew at full speed to Montpellier Hospital.

1

———

"Are you trying to kill her?" Tariq na Hassir, the formidable ruler of the Kingdom of Avana, seized the animal handler's arm, forcing him to release the rope laced around the baby giraffe's neck.

"She has suffered enough trauma." Tariq dismissed the man with a fierce scowl that struck fear into enemies.

A slither of panic crept into the young man's hushed apology. "I am sorry your Excellency."

"Release the others from their cages," Tariq growled.

The man did not have to be asked twice. He knew from experience that the Sheikh's retribution for disobedience would be swift and merciless.

"You are safe from harm," Tariq said softly, stroking the baby giraffe's long neck with a gentleness that belied his strength.

"No one will ever hurt you again, Noor," he said softly, impulsively naming her as his fingertips swept through the calf's fur. He let his long supple fingers linger a moment upon her tail. Thankfully they had saved her in time, he thought as he reached for the reins, clenching his powerful hands around the soft leather.

The rage he had first felt on hearing about the ruthless murder of the new born's mother still roared through him. Had she been executed to pay a tail dowry to the father of some money-mongering bride, he wondered? Or did some heinous person pay thousands of dollars for a wretched fly swatter?

Noor looked up and met Tariq's dark gaze. In her innocent eyes, he saw her despair, her disillusionment, her disgust with humanity. He recognized her trauma as though it was his own. Because it was.

"Humans," he said, his voice marinated with contempt. "The people you should be able to trust, the people who say they care, the people whose actions should be driven by love—the majority are driven by nothing but selfishness, deception, and lies."

Taking a bottle of milk, he placed the teat to Noor's lips. The calf's silky black lashes grazed her cheeks as she gazed down at the foreign object then looked back at Tariq. She stared silently up at him, her eyes moist and bewildered.

Tariq had trained himself to shut down his emotions but that skill suddenly failed him. His chest trembled with suppressed rage knowing the orphaned baby would never again taste her mother's milk.

"What passes for love among some people is abhorrent," he said in a low, strained voice. "On behalf of humanity, I apologize."

The killing of the calf's mother and three other rare Kordofan giraffes by trophy hunters seeking their tails further motivated the Sheikh's commitment to transform his anger into action.

"Do you really think you can save her?"

Tariq looked at Anwar, his younger brother by 11 months. His head was slightly bowed but he could see his eyes were fixed in sadness and longing.

Tension ripped down Tariq's spine. "Our father's reign of terror and tyranny have robbed Avana of prosperity and peace. I will make it my personal mission to right the injustices of the past. War and hostility must end. And it starts with how we treat those most vulnerable."

His fingers shook as he gripped the bottle of milk as Noor, at last, began to suckle.

An eerie silence swept across the precipitous

landscape of Avana's Tiwa oasis. Tariq lifted his gaze to the horizon. The only movement visible to his naked eye was the wind etching a delicate furrow as it crawled over the golden dunes.

"Not only will I provide a sanctuary for hunted wildlife and orphans like Noor, but I will liberate God's most precious creatures from the many closing zoos and other inhumane habitats around the world," he glanced over at the other animals being unloaded from the custom-built crates.

"I will create a world-acclaimed sanctuary, impenetrable by those with impure and malicious hearts. It will be the most magical, marvelous, mesmerizingly unique place, the number one ecotourism destination in the world. I will create meaningful employment for our people, restoring their dignity, attracting millions of visitors annually and contributing billions to the economy. But more importantly, I will show the world how kindness and compassion can be turned into plutonium and change the world."

Anwar glanced at the now lush landscape and recalled how barren it had once been. With no sign of life in sight, others had found it impossible to fathom his brother's vision to transform the punishing and unforgiving conditions into a haven for so many endangered species. Yet, as with everything

Tariq turned his formidable will and mind-blowing wealth to, he had succeeded where mere mortals were destined to fail.

Anwar's heart swelled with pride as he thought of all his brother's achievements. "It's an audacious and admirable plan. And if anyone can pull it off it's you, brother. Your passion, your drive, your unrelenting ambition and pursuit of goals exceeds mere mortals. And you have the endurance and power of 13,000 Arabian horses, but aren't you setting yourself up for too much hard work? Why don't you relax? Kick back. Enjoy the fruits of your reign?" Anwar said, tossing his head in the direction of the harem. "Other men would."

"Women were our father's weakness," bitterness bled from his words. "I too once made the same mistake. I too paid the price."

There was a tense silence while Tariq lifted his gaze to the sky and studied the giant falcon circling above.

"Was it not you who once taught that your greatest weakness can also be your greatest strength?" Anwar asked.

Tariq shook his head, biting down a terse retort. "I was misled." He said, nodding his command to the animal handler lingering at a respectful distance.

He petted Noor as she was led away. "All kinds of atrocities are committed in the name of love, which is why it is the most dangerous of emotions, and why I am forever turned off to women."

2

———

Shielding his eyes from the blazing sun, Tariq looked skyward, honing in on the falcon's intense, focused gaze. The power, the force, the courage and the vision of the hunting dog of the sky inspired him. And unlike humans falcons were loyal —a quality Tariq valued above all else.

"The best time for a man is the time he spends with his family," he said, glancing toward his brother. "My people are my family. My animals are my family. You are my family," he said, patting his brother's shoulders.

"The first responsibility of a leader is to make his people happy and then to provide them with the required security, stability, comfort, progress and development to ensure their survival. My loyalty is to you all."

Tariq's head jerked backward sharply as he recalled the brutal tyranny of his father. "Besides what sort of man doesn't want to care for his family? Only an ego-driven tyrant like our father would turn a blind eye to the plight of our people and the cruelty imposed on God's creatures."

Tariq gritted his teeth, his jaw locking against the strain of suppressing his emotions. There was no point voicing the hostility he felt toward his father. There was no purpose in reminding his brother that his father was a behemoth, a beast, a toxic mix of oppressiveness and evilness who had wielded monstrous power and made their lives a misery.

"This has to be the most isolated place in the world," Anwar muttered, gazing out forlornly at the neutrals and as-far-as-the-eye-can-see block tones of the desert. "No wonder mother fled to London."

While Tariq missed his mother deeply he didn't share his brother's despair. He was a thirty-six-year-old ruler who was pouring his power, his infinite wealth, his heart and soul into the land and the animals who he now offered sanctuary. He was a king filled with purpose.

"There is a lot of anti-Islamic sentiment in the world. People believe we are a nation of murderers. Thanks to people who corrupt our ways for their evil agenda. Thanks to our father and his violent, corrupt rule. Thanks to warlords and governments who seek to profit from war and spread their lies. Because of all these things the international community fears us. They have been driven away. I want to bring people back here. I want to restore our nation's pride. I want to show the world the beauty and kindness of true Islam. Our people have suffered enough shaming and violence."

"Again, you have set yourself a formidable task. Are you sure you're not throwing yourself into this audacious cause just to forget about your disobedient wife?"

"My ex-wife," he corrected. His brief marriage had been a disaster. He should have resisted the arrangement. He should have refused to cement his father's power-base by marrying the daughter of his pugnacious uncle.

Loyalty. That was Tariq's weakness. Loyalty, to family, no matter the personal cost.

The marriage was as archaic as it was disastrous. But that didn't stop Tariq wanting a family—one that didn't place demands on him he wasn't equipped to keep.

Duty—that's what counted.

The irony didn't escape him. Duty had claimed his marriage. He knew Fatima took other lovers, just like he knew that some people weren't suited to marriage. But he also knew that if he hadn't been more married to his people and his quest than he'd ever been to his wife, he might have prevented her from escaping in the night with his bodyguard in a run-down-old jeep. He might have prevented her from being buried in the sandstorm that led to her death.

He gazed out at the stark, undulating desert landscape. If he had to atone for his sins, he'd rather do it out here where there was nothing but the eerie silence and the hot wind surfing over the dunes. Where there was nothing other than his rescued wildlife meandering over what felt like the plains of the Serengeti. Where there was nothing but the blazing desert, the sand beneath his toes, and the endless Arabian sea cutting them off from the world.

Duty required sacrifice.

Tension knotted his gut as his mind drifted to the woman who angered him most. *Melanie Jones.* It had been her fault his older brother, Zayed had abdicated, and Tariq had been catapulted into the role of ruler.

Tariq vowed long ago that while he loved his older brother dearly, his disloyalty had cost too high a price. He had vowed, no matter how painful, he would never speak or think of them again.

Tariq ran his fingers down the dark brown back feathers of the hawk. "He who wants to advance should always look ahead," he said, turning to his younger brother.

"There are worse things than an eternity spent in this beautiful kingdom of islands, miles away from anything, draped in wind and quiet, sand-storms and hot desert breezes. Anchored between the majestic desert and surrounded by the shimmering Arabian sea. You will understand the preciousness of this gift soon enough, Anwar."

The Kingdom of Avana had been the crown in the jewel of Tariq's ancestors since time began. Only this time, under his rule, instead of bloody and catastrophic wars provoked by his father's oppressive regime the Kingdom of Avana would enjoy a reign of prosperous peace.

And he'd dedicate himself to his cause—and none other. Because when he looked around Tariq didn't see the life-sentence his younger brother Anwar imagined or the chokehold his older brother Zayed felt.

He saw his home.

Yet, while he wasn't given to despair he could see his future as well as anyone if he continued alone. Today's reclusive hermit is tomorrow's bitter, old relic, he told himself, as the falcon left his arm and flew toward the object of his ardent desire.

As he watched as the giant bird of prey courted a female falcon with acrobatic displays of daring aerial feats, he was acutely aware that a kingdom wasn't a kingdom with only a king to rule. To avoid Avana falling into the clutches of his father's tyrannical offspring he needed an heir.

The possibility was as outrageous as it was urgent. To bear an heir he needed a wife. The whole idea was impossible. Once betrayed, a thousand times wiser, he reminded himself.

His dark brows curved into a frown as he saw his bodyguards gallop on horseback away from the towering walls of the palace toward him.

His body tensed with the stillness of a wild animal whose every sense was alert, suspicious and wary as they approached.

"Your Excellency! Come quickly. There's been an accident."

3

"Please, please, please choose me," Melanie Jones prayed inwardly. She swallowed hard, an ache building in her chest, as she checked her watch, then checked again as she paced the floor outside the Council administrative offices in central London. She heaved a deep breath as her thoughts raced.

Six minutes until her fate would be decided. She checked her watch again. Five minutes, 59 seconds until the officials from The Council and the other key teams assessing her architectural design for the new community library would decide her fate.

Had she done a good enough job to convince them to sign off her concept for the project? The newly elected bureaucrats in the state government had challenged her design and costings, and the whole concept was in danger of coming to a crashing end.

Had she conceded too much when she yielded to their demands to rein in her vision?

Just for once she wished she could shrug off the stigma that dogged her when time after time, despite her award-winning designs, none of her buildings were ever constructed.

Just once she wished the vision she saw, the beauty she visualized, the joy she knew would be felt by those who eventually inhabited her buildings, was shared by those with access to the vault of money needed to bring her designs into reality.

If she could just get the dammed bureaucrats to say 'yes'. Until then she'd be nothing but a paper architect. Her life's work nothing but drawings and dreams.

Dreams.

Melanie rubbed her temple, erasing the one dream she had promised herself to forsake. *She was not going to think of him.*

Her ebony-black brows knitted in a fierce line as she forced her mind to the task at hand. She glanced down at the scatter of sketches splayed across the boardroom desk, feeling a mix of awe and pride—and aloneness.

Despite the fact that her design was breath stompingly beautiful, and searingly exquisite, her concept was also daringly innovative. The sweeping feminine curves confronted many people's sense of what architecture was and what it wasn't.

While she did everything in her power to minimize her own feminineness, in her designs aggressive masculine lines, straight edges and harsh corners were resolutely banished.

Dispelled were the sharp, angular lines and boxy shapes that so many in her field admired for their cost efficiencies. Eradicated were the shapes and forms that looked more like watchtowers in the worst of the concentration camps. Welcomed were the soaring sweeps and sensuous curves that inspired and nurtured and united people regardless of race, gender, or belief.

Melanie slid her palms over the stiff folds of her shapeless noir-black upside-down jacket. The touch of tarpaulin did an adequate job of disguising her generous breasts, but even this wouldn't detract from what many considered to be her biggest failing.

She was a woman. A woman competing in a man's world.

People, she knew only too painfully, didn't like breaking with tradition. And they didn't like change.

And they most definitely didn't like a woman telling them what to do.

Everyone had told her that convincing these officials as with all other decision-makers she had to influence would take more than skill and strength of purpose. She was the outsider, just as her buildings were. On the edge, confronting other people's notions of compliance and predictability and subservience.

She'd stayed late at her office working through the night as she always did. She was quietly confident, but it was an audacious design. Why couldn't she do what her mother had always told her to do— why couldn't she settle for less?

The community library was the biggest project she and her small team of fledgling architects had ever handled—and the most important. Books changed lives. Books made people better citizens. Books liberated people from their constrained lives.

Liberation. Freedom. Escape. She owed it to people. Her architecture was designed for everyday men and women—not the elite.

She had worked on the concept tirelessly, sacrificing the rest of her life. Architecture was her big love. *Her only love.* Work kept her guilt, and her anger and her shame at bay, she told herself ignoring the emptiness and longing that slopped in her belly, calling her a liar.

. . .

CLAIMED BY THE SHEIKH, book two in the True Love series **available now from all good bookstores.**

This book is licensed for your personal enjoyment only. This book may not be re-sold or given away to other people. If you would like to share this book with another person, please purchase an additional copy for each recipient.

Published by

Blue Orchid Publishing

New Zealand

Visit www.molliemathews.com to read more about all our books and to buy them. You will also find features, author interviews and news of author events, and you can sign up for e-newsletters so that you're always first to hear about our new releases.

 Created with Vellum

ABOUT THE AUTHOR

MOLLIE MATHEWS writes fun, sophisticated, passion-filled contemporary romance. She is known for her "sensual, beautiful, empowered stories enveloped in true romance" (5-star review). Her books have resonated with a global audience. She has been featured in magazines, television, and radio.

A former child and family therapist Mollie passionately believes in the power of romance to transform people's lives. She loves Mother Theresa's words, *"We are all pens in the hands of a writing God sending love letters to the world."*

Her stories are unashamedly positive, optimistic, full of fun and passion.

She is graduate of Victoria University, in Wellington, New Zealand and has given keynote speeches at romance writers conventions and international seminars.

Mollie follows the sun, dividing her time between New Zealand and exotic locations—wherever she intends setting her next romance novel. She lives with her very own romantic hero, Lorenzo—tall, dark, terribly handsome and fluent in Spanish!

Follow her on BookBub https://www.bookbub.com/authors/mollie-mathews and on her blog https://molliemathews.wordpress.com

and sign up for Mollie's newsletter at www.Molliemathews.com and receive her FREE gift.

Follow Mollie on twitter at www.twitter.com/molliemathewsnz

Join Mollie on Facebook at www.facebook.com/molliemathewsnz

Be inspired by Mollie on Instagram www.instagram.com/molliemathewsauthor

Check out her inspiration board on Pinterest www.nz.pinterest.com/molliemathews/

Writing as Cassandra Gaisford (www. cassandragaisford.com), she is also an award-winning artist and bestselling author of self-empowerment books. Cassandra is celebrated by her readers as, "The Queen of Uplifting Inspiration."

BY MOLLIE MATHEWS

GEMSTONE BILLIONAIRE BRIDES:

THE ITALIAN BILLIONAIRE'S CHRISTMAS BRIDE

THE ITALIAN BILLIONAIRE'S SCANDALOUS MARRIAGE

GEMSTONE BILLIONAIRES 2 BOOK-BUNDLE BOX SET

GEMSTONE BILLIONAIRES 3 BOOK-BUNDLE BOX SET

PASSION DOWN UNDER:

MARRIED BY CHRISTMAS
BRIDE OF GOLD

TRUE LOVE:

FLIGHT of PASSION
CLAIMED by THE SHEIKH

***PASSION DOWN UNDER SASSY
    SHORT STORIES:***

TWIST OF FATE
LOVE ME FOREVER
LOVE ME AS I AM
FOREVER AND ALWAYS
THE LIGHTKEEPER'S LOVER
*PASSION DOWN UNDER 2 BOOK-
    BUNDLE BOX SET (Books 1 & 2)*